Sin City Wolf

HOWL

JANUARY BAIN

Howl
ISBN # 978-1-83943-954-4
©Copyright January Bain 2021
Cover Art by Claire Siemaszkiewicz ©Copyright January 2021
Interior text design by Claire Siemaszkiewicz
Totally Bound Publishing

HOWL

Dedication

Thank you for taking the time to read my story in this
busy world. I appreciate it more than you can know.
A special thanks to my esteemed publisher, Claire, for
her awesome support with this sparkling new novel
and forthcoming series that I am so excited to share
with all of you.
To Rebecca, my brilliant editor — as always bless you
for making my stories shine.
Many thanks to all the staff and writers at Totally
Bound Publishing for their wonderful support and help.
To my very own White Knight, Don. How can a
simple thank you ever be enough? It's an honor to be
with you. All my love, always.

Chapter One

Cristaldo

I stared out at the night, the pull of the waxing moon yanking hard. Taking a gulp of my Dalmore 62, the finest single malt whisky ever produced, I raked a hand through my hair. The need to run free was building, growing stronger by the hour. I ached to let the clean, dry desert wind blow everything else away.

Blame it on the blood moon, an ominous portent to all my wild forbearers, scheduled to rise over Las Vegas's towering skyline in a matter of days. All my billions couldn't stop that trickster from wreaking havoc on my kind. Not that I would trade places with any otherworldly creature. *Nothing beats being a werewolf. Nothing.* Especially being a billionaire werewolf, with more money and possessions than any other wolf — and most humans — on the planet.

I savored the final gulp of the fragrant whisky with its drumroll and smooth finish. It would prove amusing to see what my rivals at the House of Ribelle had planned during the event, necessitating me showing those mongrels their low rank in the pecking order. My wolf bristled at the very idea, prepared to strike.

I dropped my glass onto the proofs of the recent interview I'd done for *Business Leader Quarterly*. The founding of the Royal Bank of Luceres and the recent expansion of our casino enterprises into several new countries was the stuff of legend and warranted a huge center spread in the magazine. Amusing really, humans being unable to see even that which what was right in front of their noses. My photo stared from the piece, all *GQ* to the public, but the slick surface hid a beast, one ready to burst forth at a moment's notice.

And that beast, bored and weary at the sameness of the days, needed a change. Where was the excitement? The new challenge? Having gathered all the riches the world had to offer didn't fill the deep void of longing, growing stronger by the day, of wanting something more. Only to myself would I admit that my life was lacking, that surrounded by so many, I was lonely.

Maybe it was time to choose a mate? Even if she wasn't the famed Forever Mate so valued by the pack, at least I would have company at night. Someone to share my victories with. *No.* I wanted the real thing. A true mate at my side, anointed as being the chosen one of destiny. I raised my head and closed my eyes, catching a sense of change on the wind. Something was coming…

Thud.

My office door slammed wide open, causing a low growl of warning to escape my throat before I caught sight of the intruder who'd broken my concentration. *Ah, Lucius. My identical twin.* He'd come bearing dubious gifts, by the look of it.

Two frightened young women preceded my brother inside the penthouse offices of the Glitter Palace casino. *They should be scared.* Lucius might have been named for the light, but his heart was filled with darkness.

"I caught this pair skulking about, asking the dealers questions about our operation and generally making a nuisance of themselves. I intervened when they bribed one of our staff into letting them into the restricted area…bribed with the promise of a free blow job."

"That's not fair," the taller of the pair objected. They were beautiful women, tall and blonde and done up in the stock-in-trade of those looking for a good time. *Or to provide one.* I raised a sardonic eyebrow at her as she continued her protest.

"I'm just a student of hotel management, trying to get some pointers from those working in the real world. My friend Brandi only came along for company. I'm Jill, by the way."

Even from twenty feet away I could smell the smoking lie that scented her skin. Normally I would tell them both to strip, to prove themselves innocent. Today, I found the idea abhorrent. Lucius gave me a strange look, waiting for my reaction. I nodded at him. *You want this, go ahead.*

"Strip."

They both stared at Lucius with huge doe-like eyes.

"What?" Jill asked, her gaze flitting back and forth between me and Lucius.

"You heard me. If you're innocent, strip," Lucius said.

"I'm not wearing a wire."

"Prove it. I'll let you leave if you're clean."

The one called Brandi shook her head. "I'm not doing this. You can't make me." She hugged both arms around her upper body.

"I can and I will. We're the only authority here at the Glit." Lucius used the shortened version of the Glitter Palace, our casino's name. His demands had aroused the taller one—her scent saturated the air with a sweet musk. My nose twitched, ambivalent about the odor.

"What's it to be, Jill? Strip or banishment?"

"So ban me. I don't care," Brandi said.

Jill looked my twin straight in the eyes, challenging him. She raised her arms in a graceful arc and undid the strings tied at the back of her neck, letting her short blue chiffon gown fall in a shimmer of fabric the length of her body to puddle on the floor. Underneath, she was naked except for a tiny pair of white lace panties. Her luscious double Ds were firm and upraised, the nipples tight and protruding out a good half inch, begging to be pinched and sucked. Apparently, Jill liked to be told what to do, like a long string of Jills before her. Bored now, my mind drifted. Even my wolf seemed to find the display less interesting than usual, just sitting back observing instead of wanting to play.

"See, no wire," she said. She twirled in a full circle, her long blonde hair cascading around her, her breasts swaying with the graceful ballet-like movements of her body.

"How about under those panties?" Lucius asked, the challenge clear. One thing we did agree on—there was nothing on earth more beautiful than the female body. But today, I sat and contemplated having another strong drink, drumming my fingers on my desktop.

She hooked her fingers into the elastic waistband and eased the panties down her long tan legs, exposing her complete Brazilian wax job. Then, slipping the lace over her four-inch platform heels, she threw them at Lucius. He caught them and took a deep whiff of their fragrant dampness. "Nice. Now you." He pointed at the other girl.

She shook her head. "No way."

I suddenly realized I'd prefer to go for a run than be here. The pent-up lust from the pull of the coming wolf moon made my skin ripple with the urge. If this female was reluctant, then banning her from the premises would suffice. Neither I nor Lucius would force a woman. Why should we, when they all came of their own accord? Not that I wouldn't mind a good chase for a change—as long as I won. *And I always win.*

"Fine. But be advised, a photo will be taken and shared with the staff," Lucius said. He was dragging this out and I wanted it over and done with. I tried to catch his eye to let him know.

The female hesitated, biting her bottom lip. I could see through the sham. I had to give it to them—the Ribelle dogs were attracting better-looking spies. Not brighter, perhaps, unless they were looking to be caught? They'd have to be checked over thoroughly before they could leave the premises. I'd leave those honors to my twin.

Lucius glanced my way, lust darkening his complexion. He, perhaps more than I, enjoyed our couplings with willing women in the immediate vicinity of the other. Our more studious younger twin brothers, currently in Rome, enjoyed having the *same* woman, but I did not imagine that ever being the case for me and Lucius, with me being alpha.

Spy number two shimmied out of her tight minidress, exposing another spectacular set of large breasts and a lack of underwear, her reluctance an obvious game. *And a lure.*

"I'll need to check you for bugs," Lucius said.

Jill, spy number one, offered herself to my brother, raising her hands high above her head in the surrender position. He caged her wrists between one of his hands, then ran his other hand through her hair, then down her supple flesh, tweaking her nipples before slipping his fingers down to her pussy. She arched her back.

From the corner of my eye, I caught the slight shimmer of the cosmic disturbance in the air around Lucius, his eyes flashing blue before returning to brown. He wanted the change. I got it. Business had been all-consuming of late, especially concluding the arrangements on the acquisition of the new bank.

A loud knock sounded at the door. "Come in," I called.

"Sorry to bother you, sire," Serge said with all due respect.

My right-hand man, second in line after Lucius and similar to a mafia don's *consigliere*, looked unusually agitated, though he was doing an admirable job of attempting to hide it. But *my* job was to miss nothing that might affect those I was in charge of. Every little nuance meant something.

"Yes?"

"Just advising you that the all-girl band, The Sirens, has arrived and is set up in Nero's." Serge was fully aware of my standing order to make sure I knew *everything* going on in my casino. The online contest we'd run for the chance to win three nights' playing at Nero's had drawn a lot of media attention—good for business, and good for the group that would benefit from the exposure.

I nodded. The sense of change in the wind tonight grew stronger. *Time to pay close attention*, it seemed to say.

The lights in the room dimmed. My twin was making preparations to fuck the women.

"Check their jewelry, Lucius. Remember the last time." Hiding a bug in an earring had worked until I'd had the penthouse swept for electronic devices.

I made a quick decision in the moment, born of my urge to get out of the office and check on the band that had drawn so much attention.

"Let's go," I said to Serge.

I led the way to my private elevator across the hall and punched the lobby number. We rode in silence, my wolf somewhat annoyed about losing out on the easy tail waiting upstairs in my office, now that I had chosen to move on. But my mind went back to thoughts of my own Forever Mate and what that would mean in my life.

I shook my head with finality, pushing the idea away. The chances of that happening after all this time were slim to none. But that didn't mean I couldn't enjoy the company of a female, under the right circumstances, to keep the urges at bay.

Moon madness is a bitch.

Chapter Two

Everly

"Pinch me! I can't believe we're here, set up and ready to have at it!" Cleo screamed, making me wince. Of late my hearing seemed to be keener than ever — surprising, really, since I'm a drummer in a band who doesn't bother with hearing protection.

"Oh, we're doing it all right." I resisted the urge to actually pinch her. Her over-the-top enthusiasm left me uncomfortable. If calm waters ran deep, then I must have been a bottomless lake. The only time I came alive was playing the drums and losing myself in the driving beat. The sense of being insulated from the world was amazing. But in all honesty, I wanted this opportunity even more than Cleo, though for entirely different reasons. She wanted fame, but I wanted my family to have a better life, to pay them back for all their faith in me.

Cleo put her hands on her curvy hips and frowned at me. "Well, you could show a little appreciation for that fact. Look, Layla's happy about it." She pointed at the third member of our all-girl band.

Layla was practicing one of her spectacular ballet moves around the base of a giant marble statue of a warrior preparing to draw his sword. Her fair hair with pink highlights, in contrast to Cleo's rich auburn and my own ebony, was bouncing on her thin shoulders. Nero's, the venue we stood in, reminded me of a Roman coliseum. Ornate pillars and life-like statues defined the edges of all four walls, which were decorated with murals of Italy's vast countryside. Overhead, the representation of a night sky, with a multitude of tiny lights standing in for the stars and arranged in exact replicas of different constellations, near took my breath away. It looked that freakin' real.

The center section of the immense convention space was filled with row upon row of seating, though plush and well-spaced out for concert goers. But the best part had to be the amazing raised stage, surreal and fairy-tale-like with its backdrop of glittery silver-white icicles that had an otherworldly appearance. Our instruments were in position, with us having already completed our sound check and rehearsal an hour earlier.

The sudden realization that we'd be playing here in less than two hours hit me. A wave of heat flashed through me, accompanied by a jittery sensation. *Crap.* Was I going to be able to do this? I didn't experience stage fright often, but the posh setting felt intimidating to a girl raised in a middling-sized city in Canada.

The sound of footsteps took my attention away from the butterflies doing a frenzied tango in my stomach. Two men strode toward us. One was the manager, Serge, who we'd spoken to earlier about thanking the owner of the Glitter Palace, and the other…a giant of a man.

My pulse spiked. A Roman gladiator dressed in black Armani. A vision right out of a history book. Thick black hair combed straight back from a far-too-handsome face. Long, thick eyelashes around creamy brown eyes that must have been the envy of every woman alive. A set of cheekbones borrowed from the knife drawer. *And* a mouth as full and sensuous as sin. My lady parts tingled with new awareness. What would it be like to be manhandled by such a man? *Manhandled? When have I ever wanted to be manhandled?*

The powerful gladiator towered over me, his dark eyes glittering with an emotion I could only guess at. I barely noticed my bandmates coming up to flank me.

"Mr. Cristaldo Luceres, I'd like you to meet The Sirens, the band that won our musical contest. Cleo Ashton on guitar and vocals, Layla Bello on bass and Everly Affini on drums. Also, Everly's the songwriter of the group. They wanted to thank you, sire," Serge said with extreme deference and a bow of his head.

Sire? Are we in medieval times? But just imagine this alpha male taking charge of things in the bedroom. My body flushing with suffocating heat, I raised both hands to sweep my waist-length hair up and away from my hot, perspiring neck and into a ballet bun that Layla had taught me to do. I was all fingers, fumbling at a job I usually found quick and easy, but finally pinned the mass in place with a tortoiseshell clip that I hastily pulled from the pocket of my sundress. *There. Better.* It was a good thing I had applied a dash of deodorant this morning.

Was that a growl?

Cristaldo held out his hands toward me first and I had no choice but to touch him.

His hands swallowed mine, owing to the sheer size of his rough paws. The electricity that sparked sizzled through me, incinerating my panties. He stood even closer now, and the fragrance of the open sky and desert washed over me. I was transported back to nature, and it called and thrummed along my veins, releasing a surge of excitement that defied explanation.

"Hello, sir," I managed to squeak, before wanting to bash myself over the head for being submissive. The last thing I wanted was to let a guy think I was easy. *I'm not.* And after the last asshole I dated, Jason Stubbs, who had neglected to share with me that he was a member of the Satan's Devils motorcycle club *and* a certifiable psychopath, I needed to keep things straight.

He ran his tongue over his bottom lip, and I swallowed, mesmerized, forgetting all about Jason and the current restraining order kept safe in the bottom of my purse. That was one of the reasons I wanted this gig — putting twelve hundred miles between us. I had big hopes it would be enough.

"Hello, Everly," he said and I shuddered at the rumbling baritone that swept through me like quicksilver. He had a voice that would make a virgin weep on the way to the nunnery, all low and throaty. I could only imagine what he would sound like singing in a smoky honky-tonk. Every woman in the place would be in heat in a nanosecond.

Fortunately, my bandmates came to the rescue, quickly making small talk about how happy we all were to be there. I tried to remember a time when my nerves had been jumpier, but failed. *Get a grip. You've met hot guys before in this business. Yeah, but never one this freakin' hot. Or dangerous.* A raging inferno existed inside him, heat and charisma rolling off him in waves that could swamp a person's defenses if they weren't careful.

"I look forward with pleasure to hearing you play this evening, Miss Affini. I've been informed your drumming is quite excellent. Your name — it's of Italian heritage?"

It took a full second before I realized that Cristaldo had directed the question solely at me. I'd been so caught up in trying to understand my attraction, and my heartbeat echoed in every part of my body.

I swallowed, nodding and stumbling over the explanation, flitting my gaze from spot to spot to avoid looking at him. "Yes, both sets of grandparents emigrated from southern Italy to Surrey, British Columbia — that's in Canada — back in the seventies. My family owns Mama's Pizza. Ah, we share a border with Blaine, Washington. That's how I met Cleo and Layla, playing at a bar and looking to replace their drummer who'd abandoned them in the middle of a set. And the rest is history." The vivid memory of the auspicious occasion came to mind and made me smile. *Talk about serendipity.*

And that was the exact second my hastily done-up locks decided to part ways with the confining clip. It flew off, striking the marble floor with a sharp *twang*. I whirled around to make a grab for it and bumped into a solid body.

"Ow," I complained. I swept the escaping strands of hair back from my sweaty forehead and rubbed the spot.

"Are you all right?" Cristaldo asked. He held the clip in one hand.

"Fine." I reached to take it from him, but he held on to it.

"Turn around," he said, or rather *demanded* in that throaty tone that left me trembling again.

"What?"

"I'll fix it for you."

Before I could protest, he tugged me closer and twirled me around, then gathered all the thick sections of my long hair into his large hands. Chills swept through me. His scent entered my body, enticing me with each breath as he caressed my scalp in long, soothing strokes. I wanted to purr, to rub up against him, and closed my eyes, savoring the sensation of being looked after. He had magic hands.

It took a few minutes before I realized we were alone, that it had grown deadly quiet around us. I opened my eyes to find the rest of the group had moved off. They were huddled up on stage, discussing something.

I jerked awake as if from a trance and blushed so hot I thought I had combusted into flames. Could I have been more pitiful, letting a complete stranger do whatever it was Cristaldo had done to me? *Crap.* My panties were damp to drenching. *Damn his sensuous fingers all to hell.*

I knew he was aware of my fully aroused state the second our glances met. *Predatory. Arrogant. Dangerous.* Smoldering bedroom eyes stared back into mine, scorching hot in their intensity.

Raising a trembling hand to my hair, I found it smooth and the clip locked in place. I instinctively pressed my other hand against my lower stomach that was clenching with the urgent need to be entered and taken, preferably rough and hard and often. The image rose front and center in my mind. *What the hell?* This had never happened to me before and I had no idea how to handle it.

"How do you know how to do that? Fix hair? Did you take a hairstyling course or something?" I asked, half-joking to take my mind off other things.

I caught a flash of something in his eyes — pain — torment? I wasn't certain a second later.

"I used to fix my baby sister's hair before school. She insisted I did it better than either of her nannies."

"You're good at it."

"Strange, I haven't thought of that in years."

"Do you have other siblings?" I asked. "Me, I'm all on my lonesome. And coming from an Italian family, well, you can only imagine the pressure on me to succeed, marry then have a passel of kids."

"Two of my brothers are away at university. Alessandro and Maximus, scholars affiliated with La Sapienza, a university in Rome. Lucius works here at the casino."

He leaned down toward me and whispered seductively in my ear, the heat of his breath searing the delicate skin on my neck. My breasts felt swollen and heavy, the nipples aching, begging to be touched. "We've got some time before the show, *la mia piccola bambola*. I can take real good care of you — anything you want, I'm more than ready to provide. I can make love until the sun comes up if that would make you happy."

What? La mia piccola bambola? I'm no one's little doll! Anger at my stupidity broke through my paralysis. No way was a man going to control me. To seduce me into being something I wasn't. *Never. Again.*

I did what any self-respecting woman would do — I attacked, even though I'd never been more turned on in my life. That realization only fueled the flame.

"I'm not cheap! I don't know what you did to me just now — some kind of weird voodoo shit — but I'm telling you, I'm not having it. Leave me the hell alone!"

Doing an abrupt about-face, I stormed off to join my sisters-of-another-mother on stage.

Chapter Three

Cristaldo

Angry at the ridiculous rejection, I crooked a finger at Serge, who rushed over to join me, arriving near breathless. She would never escape me. She had just made me want her all the more, imagining bending that will to my own...with a proper spanking. Why deny herself what I knew she wanted, needed, under all that sass? The wildest, most satisfying lust known on earth is an alpha-wolf pairing.

But why this sudden drive to be with this particular female? My interest was way out of proportion. What was really going on? A possible truth dawned. Was this her? *Amico mio per sempre, mi complete.* The one who would make my life complete? *My Forever Mate.* The realization tore through all my defenses. Was I prepared for all the changes she would bring? Memories of past mates who'd found this binding connection gave me clarity. Her arrival would turn my whole world upside down. *Everything* would be different going forward.

"Yes, sire?" Serge's dark eyebrows knitted together with concern as he took in my scowl.

"What do we know about her?" I barked. My wolf snarled with frustration. *Take her. She's ours.*

"We're working on it as we speak. Did you pick up on anything? You seemed to be getting along famously for a few minutes there." He looked worried and I shouted at my wolf to stand down. It was all I could do not to run after the female and haul her away. *Worry about lawsuits later.*

Then I remember my father's sage advice on leadership and tempered my response. But *oh cazzo*, I wanted this female in my bed.

"The instant-attraction box can be checked, if that's what you're asking. But it's fine. She has a lot of spunk, that one. I hate spunk." I quirked an eyebrow at him.

Serge chuckled nervously. "She'll need it, you know, being in the music industry and all."

'Leaders have a heavy obligation to control themselves when and where possible, my son.' The exact words of my father, but tough advice to follow when my cock was as hard as steel and I wanted to pin my female to the ground and make love to her until she begged for mercy. And she *was* mine. Every fiber of my being was screaming that I had to have her. What had gone wrong? No woman had *ever* turned me down. She'd been soaking wet for me—the scent of her arousal, a sweet mix of pure sunshine and grassy meadows, still clung to me.

I stared at the confounding female standing on the stage with her bandmates and narrowed my eyes. Did she want to be romanced? Was that the problem? I couldn't remember the last time I had romanced a woman. I was my pack's alpha and women begged *me* to have them. *And now la mia piccola bambola thinks she can just shut me out?*

Something must have happened, because the woman who had my wolf riveted and ready for the chase and take-down left the stage, the other females running after her.

I strode over to intervene. "What's the problem?"

"She won't play. Says she's leaving! Do something!" the one called Cleo shouted at me.

"Everly Affini. *Stop.*"

She turned round and faced me, crossing her arms over her perfect breasts. The fragrance of her arousal washed over me again, nearly ending all my restraint, pushing me over into The Hunger. *That damn hunger, the urge to fuck with a willing partner near the full moon time, no matter their ancestry or status.* Add that to the fact she was most definitely my Forever Mate, and the pull was that much greater. The waxing blood moon crafted too much black magic. I needed to stay in control, hard as it was, to avoid detection. Putting my pack at risk was not an option.

"I won't stay here. I don't feel safe."

"What? Not safe!" I barked. "You could not *be* safer."

She shot a look at me, her lips pressed tightly together. It was then I caught a whiff of fear on her skin.

"You have my word no one will touch you in my casino."

"Not even you? After what you said with that cheesy come-on line?" she dared to ask, her cheeks bright with two spots of color. I couldn't help but admire that my female was even more gorgeous when she was angry.

"Not even me." It was only a matter of time anyway. She wanted me. Under the anger and fear, I could still detect her arousal. Maybe she was frightened by how lustful she had become? She was very young and innocent and had probably never felt that overwhelming passion in her life before.

She stood silent and considered my words. "Okay. But you stay away from me." She pointed her finger right at me. I had the urge to take it into my mouth and give it a sharp nip. I resisted, though my wolf sat up and begged. He wanted to nip her all over. To make her his.

Serge gasped. Never had he heard a woman defy me. I had to admit, she intrigued me. It took courage to decide to leave. To give up on such an opportunity. Most women I'd met would have done almost anything to play here with me.

"Thank you again, Mr. Luceres," Cleo said before shepherding her bandmates toward the door. I presumed they were headed to change into their performing outfits.

I nodded, watching Everly leave. "Find out what's going on."

"Of course, sire." Serge hurried away.

My cell phone rang. "Yes," I barked, answering it.

"If you want some action, bro, you'd better get up here fast. I've just about done them both in," Lucius said, triumph riding high in his voice.

"Not now. You let them go when you're done. I've got more important things to take care of."

Silence greeted my words. This was not something he'd heard me say before.

"Fine. But you're missing out."

I ended the call and considered my options. An idea came to mind even as my wolf howled with pent-up frustration. I had no idea how long I could keep *him* under control, twenty-first century or not.

Chapter Four

Everly

"What happened between you and that guy? What did he say, exactly, that got you so upset?" Cleo asked in the elevator, jabbing the tenth-floor button with an impatient finger.

I pressed my lips together. I didn't want to spoil the day that had begun with such high hopes. The elevator doors shut with a *whoosh* and we moved smoothly upward.

"Nothing. I don't want to discuss it now, okay? This is the moment we've talked about for so long. Let's just get our clothes and head down to prepare for the concert. We don't want to be late for our debut." We were booked in at Nero's for three glorious nights. I didn't want to think about how that was going to work with Mr. Thinks-he's-god's-gift-to-women on the prowl.

"Right. We're expected on stage in fifty-seven minutes," Layla said in her precise manner. It must have come from the years of discipline necessary to study ballet. My own background was not all that different—Italian parents hell-bent on me making something of myself. "Let's focus on what's really important. Gearing ourselves up to put our best selves out there."

"Fine. But you haven't heard the end of this. I want to know *exactly* what he said later. He may appear all James-Bond cool and sexy on the outside, but inside, he could be all dark and dangerous."

"I could see jumping his bones," Layla said, surprising me.

Cleo gave her a slanted look.

"What? Just stating the truth," Layla added. "That guy could have any woman he wanted with a crook of a finger, he's that smoking hot. Like an ancient warrior or warlord."

"He's something, all right. Trust me. The guy's just too full of himself," I said

We parted at the door to Layla's suite and I continued down to my own. I was impressed that we'd been given individual rooms after I checked on the cost of a one-night stay at the Glitter Palace. *Shocking. Enough to buy groceries for a week back home.*

I closed the door, grateful to be alone, took a full, deep breath and let it out slowly. What had just happened? Had I turned into the biggest slut since we'd left Canada? Here I was, just ready to jump into bed with a guy who acted like a big bad wolf. Cristaldo was far more macho and dangerous than Jason had ever been, and he'd been a handful I'd been quick to dump. Not that Jason believed I meant it. But I did.

I strode to the bathroom to freshen up. It was almost party time. My breath quickened at the thought of playing all my favorite music. This was what I lived for — who I was. I craved the experience of being the backbone of the band, forgetting everything else but the ancient tribal rhythm, the heartbeat of Mother Earth. I'd promised myself that I'd be playing music until the day I dropped. I'd use up every last bit of myself, all my energy, in the next two hours to satisfy the hungry crowd. And I could barely wait.

Thirty minutes later, we met up backstage, clothes hangers clutched in our hands. We helped one another change in the huge dressing room provided, checking that everything looked right for our debut.

"Oh *wow*, you guys look amazing," I said. And they did. We'd decided on matching little black dresses with red thigh-high, high-heeled suede boots with a three-inch gap between the hem and footwear. *I mean, this is Vegas, baby!* But I had no idea how I was going to keep from being exposed when I got in behind my drum kit. I tended to forget *everything* else, so I was wearing two pairs of red panties. And forgetting everything else — that was the ticket to freedom.

"Okay. Group hug," Cleo directed. Layla and I stepped forward and linked arms with her, heads bowed. "Thank you, Lord, for this opportunity to sing and play for these people tonight. We feel your blessing and hope to do you proud." Cleo's dad was a preacher and he'd instilled his values in his daughter…when she wasn't rebelling, that was.

"Amen." Layla and I spoke in tandem.

The announcer's voice rang out, and we ran, holding hands, onto center stage.

Loud whistles and thunderous clapping greeted our arrival. I headed to the back of the stage and my drum kit, climbing onto the throne behind the multitude of snares, tom-toms, cymbals and mics. One of the overhead bells dinged softly as if welcoming me home. Two hours of being totally myself and the wonderous anonymity of being in the background obscured by the drums. *Doesn't get any better.*

Cleo and Layla were out front, straps over their shoulders holding their guitars in place. Cleo sang lead, while Layla and I harmonized.

"Hel—lo, Las Vegas! We are proud to be here tonight playing for you. Please welcome my friend Everly on drums all the way from Canada, Layla on bass from the awesome city of Blaine, Washington and myself on vocals, also from the great state of Washington. And together we are The Sirens! *One, two, three, four—*"

And the music began, a song that resonated with most anyone and should get the crowd in the mood to just be feeling it. Or at least that was our hope when we'd decided on the set list.

Cleo stepped up to the mic and began singing the song I'd written that had turned into our anthem. It had the best drumming part ever in the entire history of the world.

"Slay your dragons and fly with me,
To Avalon to kiss the king.
Rise up! Rise up! Rise up, be free!"

Drumsticks in both hands, feet on the pedals, I clashed the cymbals with a thunderous sound, then surrendered to the beat that was taking me over completely. It resonated throughout my body, thrumming its magic into every atom I possessed. If a man could make me feel this, he'd be a god. *Or a wolf.* An image came into my mind of Cristaldo and I blinked it away fast as I could, nearly losing the beat. I recovered quickly. *Stop thinking.*

Hair flying everywhere, body bouncing to the beat, I let myself be swept away by the current to a land of pure escape. *Heaven.*

Chapter Five

Cristaldo

As Everly lost herself on stage, I clenched my hands into fists, claws digging into my palms. I fought the urge to transform, making the air around me shimmer in alarm. My eyes burned with the desire that would turn them incandescent and expose my wolf. *Che diavolo sta succedendo?* Never had I been affected like this. An alpha male always in control, was what I prided myself on being.

I couldn't wait until after the concert, though the group had just begun their set. It had to happen now. My skin rippled visibly with the need. The only way to bring back control was to give in to the wolf. I left the auditorium and took the flight of stairs from the penthouse leading to the rooftop and my favorite toy, a Bell-Boeing 609 Tilt-Rotor straight from the factory in France. I jumped in behind the controls and set a course for our nearest compound in the desert. *Ten minutes to freedom.*

No sooner had I landed the helicopter — and with the blades still rotating — than I was out and running. Mid-stride, I entered another realm, a parallel existence, invisible from Earth, and my body underwent the change. On the other side, through the shimmering portal, the sensation deepened until all my cells had transformed, aligned in a new form. Then I was back in the present, a wolf. The world had mutated to an array of colors unknown to the human eye, blacks and browns and grays with subtle shadings that my brain converted to what my human side saw — blues and greens, yellow and reds. I breathed in deeply, my olfactory nerves sharpened by the cool, dry air of the desert at night. The odor of dust among the cactus, scrub and clumps of grass filled my nostrils.

I picked up the scent of fast game and gave chase. Bounding along, the wind to my back, twisting and turning as I easily followed my prey, I savored the strength of the wolf. My large paws ate up the distance, the shadows of the Joshua trees familiar forms mimicking humans and moving past me at lightning speed as I continued my pursuit.

The scent of fear ahead span my brain out of control. My prey knew I was close. I redoubled my efforts, imagining the takedown. *The satisfaction.* Then the creature found his burrow all of a sudden and went to ground. *No matter.* I streaked by the spot, needing the run far more than the catch.

The dry land slapped against my paws and the wind sliced across my muzzle. Time had no meaning in the desert. The longer I ran, the lighter I felt. Expending such energy increased my strength, mile by mile, each muscle quivering with adrenaline.

A new scent drew my attention. *Wolf.* I swung my massive head to the east. The interloper was not of the Luceres pack. My brain sharpened and the thrill of the chase intensified. I covered ground quickly, totally focused on the enemy. I needed this, to show the curs their place.

I raced to the farthest section of my land and confronted the Ribelle dog. My fur rose as my tail bushed out behind me. He was hellbent on getting away, circling back and forth like a prisoner in a cell, preferring to cross over the electric fence rather than face me. I snarled my disdain at finding the coward trying so desperately to escape.

I launched myself at him, digging my claws deep into his hide, my muzzle going for his neck. Using my jaws, I clamped onto the back of his neck, going for the takedown. Blood, salty and thick, spurted into my mouth.

He let out a loud whine of pain and protest. I refused to let go, shaking him with all my might. More blood sprayed onto the ground, bright red drops that vanished instantly into the thirsty desert soil.

I wanted the kill, but the hound had learned his lesson. When I let him go a few minutes later, he lay down in submission, his vulnerable belly revealed to my gaze.

Go and never come back.

He slinked off with his tail curled between his legs.

Thrusting my muzzle upward, I howled my joy at the victory. The music poured from my chest, echoed across the land and soared up to the moon that was growing ever larger in the starlit sky. I owned this land, this place in time.

Satisfied, I made a full loop across the desert floor and arrived back at the helicopter that was sitting like a giant beast, waiting patiently for me in the moonlight. I shifted, donned a new set of clothes I always kept at the ready, climbed into the cockpit and set a quick course back to the casino's roofline. Ten minutes later I was headed to Nero's, one of my basic needs satiated.

I stood and watched the end of The Sirens' performance from my vantage point in the wings, though it was only Everly that drew my attention.

No words could possibly capture the magnificence and magic of Everly's drumming. She appeared otherworldly as she played, hearing something different from the rest of us. It made me want her all the more.

I'd watched many fine performances in Vegas over the years, but this—this was something in a class all its own. Pure raw energy and boundless talent fired her act, obviously fueled by hundreds of hours of practice. I had never been more turned on by a female in all my life…and that seemed to be the case for many males in attendance. My wolf and I growled in tandem. Flashes of red panties only worsened a dire situation. Pack rule number two—*the alpha always protects his mate and his offspring with his life.*

"They are good, are they not, sire? Is it any wonder they won the contest hands-down?" Serge asked, with a rare show of pleasure. He had joined me during the final moments of the concert's encore.

"Too good. Others are leering at her." My wolf wanted to pounce, to wreak mayhem on the crowd, and I contained him with great difficulty. I needed to keep absolute control. *The existence of our kind must never be revealed.* Pack rule number one. I would take myself out before harming my pack.

"Are you worried? I have added extra security tonight."

"No. Just see that the girls are escorted to their rooms when the time comes. No delays. And make sure that Everly is particularly well guarded. Whatever it takes."

"Of course."

"And see that her room is filled with all the red roses you can lay your hands on." No doubt remained in my mind that she was my genetic match, leaving only one question. Was she of dual nature, meaning she could be mated to either house? As much as we relied on DNA testing in the twenty-first century, my primal wolf didn't want to wait for confirmation. No hound from the House of Ribelle could ever be a true Forever Mate to her as I would be. My wolf wanted her and clamored for the ancient, tried-and-true method—bite and claim.

The delicious fragrance Everly sent into the air with each electrifying movement on stage was overwhelming all my defenses. But to mark her as mine before results were formally in was forbidden, as the Ribelles could challenge for her. I could only imagine the bloodbath that could ensue if I didn't follow the ancient rules. I had to keep control. I couldn't risk it. Not yet. But I would break down her defenses, one by one. No matter her genetics, we could make love—there were no laws against that. *And there's nothing I love more than a challenge.* It was how I'd managed to grow our business interests by twenty-five percent this past year alone.

"Yes, sire. I also found out she has a protection order against one Jason Wayne Stubbs of Surrey, B.C. Apparently, he's a member of the Satan's Devils bike club and into drugs, guns and prostitution. One conviction for assault."

Destroy.

I remained silent, not trusting myself to speak.

"Right. Well, I'll let you know what I find out about her blood DNA. If she's one of ours. I know how important that information is to you, so I've put an urgent request it for it to take absolute priority over any other lab work. Everly's a regular donor, due to her having a rare blood type, and I'm having a sample flown down for testing."

"I know she is meant to be mine, but good job."

Serge startled at my unaccustomed praise. "Ah, thank you, sire. There is one other item on our agenda I need to speak to you about." He hesitated. "The Lupercalia. It's in four days, to coincide with the full moon."

I groaned, though normally I looked forward to it. Three days of lust and debauchery. *No limits.* But sync that with a super blood wolf moon and trouble was bound to erupt. "Fine. But I'll need to set some ground rules this year."

"You know how they live for the chance to throw away all modern conventions. Revert to the old ways." Serge kept his tone submissive.

He spoke the truth, but it rankled to have my word questioned, though I normally encouraged the outpouring of pack wildness. The event, like New Orleans's Mardi Gras on steroids, held on my estate in the Mojave Desert with its Joshua trees and otherworldliness, satisfied and quenched ancient urges. I had an instant vision of me and Everly running wild, making love under a desert sky filled with glittering stars.

"I'll take your words under advisement." I narrowed my eyes, liking the argument that arose in my feverish brain. "Perhaps the traditional way is best. And if it is, I should just go ahead and claim her."

Serge's face reddened with my words. He pressed his lips tightly together before speaking. "I still remember very well, like it was yesterday, when my Forever Mate came into my life. I found myself in dire straits, trying to control the overwhelming urges. I pretty much wore out a five-pointed talisman in the process, to help curb the worst of the impulses. So, I understand what you're going through. The way you're reacting to her, I'm certain the lab results will confirm it. But you know, it will be up to her. If she says no to allowing her wild nature to be released, she has that right. You can't aid in turning her. Not every intended mate will embrace our life. You need to tread carefully, sire. Woo her. Take the time required. Forgive me, but I say this only for your own good."

"What happens if she denies herself what she so obviously wants?" That thought had never actually occurred to me before. I'd always taken what I wanted.

"I'd advise not telling her of our existence until you're more certain of things. Articles under pack rule one state we have to wipe her memory. We must protect knowledge of our existence at all costs."

I shuddered with distaste, remembering the final solution used in ancient times. At least today we paid vampires to do it, though no bloodsucker would ever be allowed to touch her. That way would lead to the loss of a limb, or more likely a life.

"Making love to her and claiming her are two very different things."

"Yes, but dangerous. What if your wolf takes over entirely?" he asked.

"I can handle myself."

A flash of movement drew my attention, and our conversation was instantly forgotten. My heightened wolf vision cut through the glare of stage lights that would have blinded weaker human eyes and into the audience. Hundreds of concert-goers were still sitting through The Sirens' final encore of the evening, their animated faces proving the power of the band's music. But a group of six wolves from the House of Ribelle, led by Rocco, their enforcer, was on the move, toward the stage.

"How did they get in?" I asked before jumping onto the main floor in a single leap and racing to intercept their advance.

"Wait! I'll call for backup," Serge shouted at me. I ignored him and continued my rush toward the enemy. *Protect her at all costs.*

Chapter Six

Everly

I lurched out of my trance, my body drenched in perspiration and wet strands of dark hair plastered to my cheeks. My vision widened from the narrow tunnel enclosing only my drum kit to a view of the entire concert venue. The house lights turned on and thunderous applause erupted, resounding inside my head. Cleo and Layla bowed at center stage, holding hands. *Right. I'm supposed to join them.*

More people were standing and clapping, but all I could see was a large man racing toward a group of men who were advancing on the stage.

Is that Cristaldo? A shrillness like a single out-of-tune violin note passed through me. What was going on? From the outer edges of the casino, men poured in, racing down the aisles and between marble statues. I prayed they'd reach him in time to prevent any violence.

My eyes picked up on a sort of vibration in the air, a light bluish shimmering, an explosion of energy flowing out in waves from the men involved in the confrontation. *What is this?*

But then the strange vision halted and the air cleared. The cavalry had arrived and the group of men were now surrounded by security. I breathed easier. As much as Cristaldo had upset me with his pick-up line, I didn't want to see him in any danger, though he seemed more dangerous than an entire motorbike rally of Satan's Devils bikers celebrating a new member's full patch.

The crowd didn't seem to notice the altercation — everyone still clapped, rising and standing in a thunderous ovation. My bandmates gestured madly at me. I managed to find my feet and joined my friends on center stage. We took our final bow in unison.

"Wow, we were *on fire* tonight, my fellow goddesses! Thank you! Thank you!" Cleo said, and I couldn't disagree. We had stirred up the crowd more than anticipated. Far more.

We headed backstage and I grabbed water from the refreshment table. I slugged back the whole bottle in one go. Drumming was thirsty business.

"Congratulations!" All around us, good wishes were being thrown by the excited crowd backstage who were busy toasting us. For the next few minutes, we were all kept occupied, thanking everyone for their support. Finally, we got a few minutes to speak together.

"And we get two more nights of this!" Layla gloated. Her eyes were lit up like California stars. "Just imagine. Some Nashville or Hollywood scout *must* come by in that time. This is it! We're on our way! This time next year we'll be rolling in the dough."

"Or rolling in the constant touring," I said with a groan. "You guys ready for that?"

"I was born ready!" Cleo said, her grin wide.

I pulled away from everyone, went to the edge of the curtain and peered into the crowd. Cristaldo was making his way back to the stage and he caught me in the act, his eyes boring into mine. I startled and withdrew, angry with myself for letting him catch me.

Serge entered through the wings and dashed over to us. "I need to let you know that we're providing security to make sure you all get to your rooms safely."

"Why wouldn't we?" Cleo asked, her water bottle halting on its way to her lips.

He shrugged. "It's just a precaution."

"Anything to do with the altercation I witnessed a few minutes ago?" I asked.

His eyes widened to an owl's size. "No, there's no problem. We just take security seriously here at the Glit."

"The Glit?" I asked.

His face reddened. "Excuse me, I meant the Glitter Palace." He was flustered because there was a problem, and in his extreme agitation, he'd let the name slip. *Oh yeah, we're definitely in Macho-land.*

"Tell your boss we're fine. We don't need his security people all up in our faces," I said.

"Miss Affini, I beg of you, just let us do our jobs. My sire would not forgive himself if anyone so much as harmed a hair on your head. He *particularly* requested extra security just for you."

"What about the hair on my head?" Cleo asked, her eyes narrowed. "What am I, chopped liver?"

"I want *all* of you to be safe," Cristaldo said, striding over to join us. He looked unscathed by the recent altercation. Not a single hair out of place or one wrinkle in his Armani. Yeah, Cleo was right. James Bond on the outside, but who *exactly* was on the inside? The man was intriguing, I'd give him that.

He looked me up and down slowly, devouring me with a smoldering glance. It made me feel powerful, like I was the only woman in his universe. I shook my head to clear it. *I must be imagining things.*

"We're fine. And we were just leaving," I said. I lobbed my empty water bottle into the recycling trash.

Layla gave me a look that asked, *What's the matter with you?*

Cristaldo grabbed my arm. "You will accept an escort to your room. Me or someone else. Choose."

I gave him my best *don't mess with me* look. "What's the problem now? You let some lowlife into the casino?"

"Everly! He just wants to be sure we're safe," Cleo intervened in a voice tinged with concern.

"Fine, then. I choose someone else."

"But I'm here now, *la mia piccola bambola*. I'll escort you. Keep you safe."

I narrowed my eyes at him. "Then why ask? And for heaven's sake, don't call me that! I'm not your little doll."

"What do you want me to call you? Is it my fault you look like a china doll with those emerald eyes, fair skin and dark hair?" He came closer, as if my answer held all the mysteries of the universe.

I bit my tongue to avoid a caustic reply, aided by a jab in my ribs by Cleo. "Can I talk to you for a minute?" she asked, giving me a sharp nod.

"Sure."

I followed her into the ladies' bathroom.

"What's your problem?" she asked, turning on me. "Spill. I need to make sense of this."

I hesitated, uncertain if I could articulate it for her in any way that would help her understand.

She gave me a frustrated look. "Okay, I get that he's a bit forward with you. Made some kind of pass you won't explain. But the fact remains, he seems to be quite taken with you. But why are you being so difficult in return? Just allow him to escort us back to our rooms and say goodbye. No problem-o. I mean, the guy's the hottest hunk I've ever seen. If it was me, it would be a friggin' dream come true that he was interested in this small-town girl. The guy does own this casino."

"It's not that. I just feel uncomfortable around him, okay? He turns me on too much." As soon as the words were out of my mouth, I wanted to yank them back.

"*What*? How can you be turned on too much? That's impossible."

"Trust me. It is. It doesn't feel natural. Like it's unreal or voodoo."

"You just haven't been laid in a long time. How long has it been? Since Jason, right?"

I couldn't look her in the eyes.

"I thought so. Not every guy is a dud like Jason."

"But he's pretty aggressive. What if he's just the same, you know? Shows his true colors once we've spent time together? I have a track record of choosing the wrong guy."

"We're only here for a few days. Loosen up a little. Do you good. I mean, have you really *looked* at him? He's so gorgeous he probably has females throwing their panties at him from across the street. He's got so much pussy coming at him it's falling out of his pockets."

"Enough already." I couldn't avoid a quick smile at the crazy image. Cleo had a mouth on her. *Always has had.* But she did have a point. I could easily walk away from this. Four days and I'd be back safe and sound back in Surrey, B.C. Well, maybe, if Jason managed to keep his distance.

"Okay. We good here? Will you let the bodyguard walk us to our rooms so all of us will be safe from the big bad wolf?"

I let out a deep sigh. "Okay. You win." But why did I get the funny feeling that Cristaldo was the real big bad wolf?

"Nah, you play your cards right and you'll be the winner. Time spent around that Italian hottie will be just the ticket you need to forget all about Jason. Besides, guys like Cristaldo are not the kind you marry. Just imagine him in Surrey? *Phttt.* Not going to happen. He's not built for the long haul. A few days, you both move on."

"Maybe." Were we missing something here? But I was damned if I knew what that thing was. And thinking of such a powerful man walking into our simple two-story white frame house to sit down for Christmas dinner make me want to burst into hysterical giggles.

She linked arms with me. "No *maybes* about it. I just wish he would have noticed me first. He's a smoking-hot piece. All Roger Moore cool on the outside, but you can feel his Sean Connery-ness like a volcano ready to erupt on the inside. I'd screw his brains out tonight if he looked at me the way he's been looking at you."

"You would not!" The thought put me right on edge. I might not have wanted to act on satisfying my raging libido, but I certainly didn't feel comfortable with someone else moving in and taking over. Though I imagined women lining up ready to take a man like him on. A flash of red obscured my vision for a second, startling me.

"See. You're jealous already. Hell, go for it, girl. You know you want to." A mischievous grin lit up her face. "And I'm up for a three-way, too."

"How is it you're the daughter of a preacher again?" I asked in a teasing tone, not certain I liked the direction of this conversation. I was just beginning to come down from the high the concert had created It could take hours for the jittery feeling to pass and me to sleep.

"It's not Sunday, girlfriend. It's Thursday night. And we got days to *par-tie*. And catch afternoon concerts of the performers we've always dreamed of seeing in person. You want my advice? Screw his brains out. And if you're not up for it, tell him to give me a call."

I shook my head, not sure how to answer that. "We should get back. I'm starving. Let's order room service and have an all-girls party."

"Fine. But if you change your mind, hang your panties on the doorknob. I'll know what's up. And I bet he can get it up and keep it up *all night long*." She sang the last few words in a rollicking key of C.

I laughed. "Not going happen."

She propped one hand on her hip, her lips upturned in a wide Cheshire-cat grin. "I'll make you a bet that you can't keep your hands off him. You guys will be doing the nasty, mark my words. And if I win, you owe me a bottle of champagne—the good stuff, not the cheap swill we drink because we're always broke."

"And if I win?"

"Going to bed with that handsome hunk? You already win the big one."

"Not fair. If I win, you owe me a figurine for my Howling Wolves collection." I've always had a thing about wolves. Maybe it came from living in Canada and having seen their awesome power firsthand.

"Fine. But you'll be the one out of pocket," she said.

"Not going to happen. I have a secret weapon. I may have brought a little something along to keep me company." I waggled my eyebrows at her to punctuate my words.

It took a moment for her to register what I was talking about, but it was just too satisfying to see Cleo's face turn bright pink as she choked. I patted her on the back to aid her catching her breath. It wasn't often I got to turn the tables.

"Crap, Everly, didn't expect that from you. Okay, let's get out of here. A juicy cheeseburger and fries are calling my name."

We linked arms and exited the bathroom.

Cristaldo stood right where we'd left him, his big arms folded over his massive chest, his dark eyes locked on me. He looked even hotter, more intense, and definitely more dangerous. I felt like a satellite trapped in his orbit, about to crash and burn. He wasn't the guy to be kept waiting. *By anyone.* I swallowed against the strange feelings that were rising in my body

"Are you ready now?" he asked, and I heard the underlying message — *Did your fellow band member talk some sense into you?*

"Let's go, Wolfie," I said in retaliation for being called a little doll, cutting him down to size with my steely glance even as I wondered what would it be like to kiss this man.

His eyes widened with surprise at my nickname. *Sweet. I'm nobody's plaything.* It was best he knew that.

Layla shot me a grin, but no one talked as the big bad wolf escorted us out of the area and into the elevator. My mind traveled back over the events of the concert and stalled on one important part. "What almost happened tonight? I saw a group of men looking to confront you," I asked, directing my question to the man standing protectively by my side.

"If you saw that, why did you fight me on my providing security?"

He had a point, but I didn't want to go there again. Having him stand so close in the elevator was punishment enough. It seemed every atom in my body had woken up, his very presence invading me. I dared to peek at him through my thick eyelashes. He was looking me up and down slowly, eating me up with those hungry eyes. When he moistened his lips, I almost groaned out loud. *But two can play that game, Wolfie.* I shook my head, making my long hair wave down my back, then ran a finger over the partially opened seam of my lips, my eyes promising a whole lot more.

Layla elbowed me in the side. *Accidentally?* I managed to behave myself until we walked off the elevator.

"I'll call room service," Cleo said when she stopped at her room first. "Let's all meet here after we shower, okay?"

"Sounds good. Be there soon," I said in a bright tone of voice. I turned to our self-appointed security guard. "You can go. I'll be fine."

"I'll walk you all the way." His tone commanded and I fell in beside him. Layla's room came next and she vanished inside.

Suddenly we were alone in the hallway and the realization hit me hard.

We stopped in front of my door and I removed the key card I'd stashed in my bra.

Did he just growl?

He cocked a dark slash of an eyebrow and moved in toward me, then took my face in his hands, lowering his mouth to mine. His breath, fragrant with the tantalizing scent of cinnamon, washed over me, the heat caressing my skin. I stood frozen in place. Never had I wanted a man to kiss me more.

"I want to kiss you. All over. What do you say, *la mia bella donna*?"

"Don't call me that." But my words lacked conviction. Being called a beautiful woman in Italian didn't exactly suck. I was so turned on that my knees turned to water. I managed to lay one ground rule. "Just *one* kiss. Not all over. Then we'll decide."

"But where do you want that first kiss? Here?" He touched my forehead with fingers that soothed. "Here?" He caressed my cheek with surprising tenderness. "Or here?" He slipped his hand down to my right breast and set it on fire, instantly heavy and swollen with need, the nipple tight and pleading to be chosen. Its twin followed suit, begging for the same attention.

I wanted to fight and I wanted to surrender. My common sense had abandoned me.

"On the lips, *Wolfie*." How had I managed the sass? A red warning light winked in the outer corners of my vision—*beware, entering dangerous territory.*

He lowered his mouth to mine.

He took.

Demanded.

Owned me.

I clutched at his jacket and drew him closer still, right up against my body. I breathed short bursts of air through my nose while he dived his tongue into my mouth and swept it against mine, over and over in a lustful battle of decadence and despair. It was the perfect marriage of suction and pressure, our mouths busy teaching each other. I squirmed from the sensation, rubbing my thighs restlessly against his hard length as I crashed against the hotel door. He held my head in place, giving me what he wanted and what I didn't know I needed. *So. Damn. Much.*

I moaned into his mouth.

My pussy was drenched, my panties beyond saving.

I kissed him harder, dizziness threatening to claim me. Then he pulled back slightly, both hands pressed flat against the wall on either side of my head like he didn't trust himself. His sheer size surrounded me, enticing me. I arched my back, begging him for more.

"Well?" he asked.

I hadn't a clue what he was talking about. Why he'd stopped.

"What?" All I wanted was for the kiss to continue.

"Just one kiss? Remember? Or do you want more?"

His male flesh and arousing scent of musk surrounded me, cocooning us in wild black magic. I swear the air shimmered. I blinked a few times to clear my eyes. *What the hell was I thinking?*

"That was one kiss?" I asked faintly. What if he had continued, kissed me all over? I would have combusted into a puddle of nothingness. *Pure. Pleasurable. Nothingness.*

He lowered his mouth to my ear, his voice darker, commanding.

"Don't toy with me, *piccolo tesoro*. I'm not the man to play with. I take what I want. Always have, always will. It is the way of things." Though his eyes hinted at a deeper emotion that might be sadness or loneliness, my back went up at his words. *Oh, now I'm his little sweetheart, am I?*

"Maybe in your world, *Wolfie*. Not in mine."

Quick footsteps advanced down the hallway and saved me from further discussion.

My big bad wolf stepped back and turned toward the person coming at us.

"Hey, bro, I've been looking all over for you."

I caught sight of the speaker and froze. An exact replica of Cristaldo had magically appeared.

"Lucius. What are you doing here?"

Right, one of the brothers. The newcomer glanced my way before answering. His eyes widened slightly and a frown appeared between his dark eyebrows. He moved forward and sniffed the air, a strange move that had me taking a step backward. What was his deal? Was he on coke? That was the only explanation that came to mind for a person sniffing so rudely like that.

"Who are you?" he demanded. It was then that I realized the two men, obviously identical twins, were vastly different. This one, Lucius, had edgier eyes, and a darker spirit swam in their depths, accompanied by a cruel-looking mouth. Wolfie might be the alpha male, but his lofty status was tempered by intelligence and a glimpse of some deep emotion I had caught sight of after we'd kissed. I instinctively did not trust this new doppelganger.

"This is Everly Affini," Cristaldo said. He looked displeased by the interruption. "Everly, meet my brother, Lucius. Who's just about to leave."

"Cristaldo, is that any way to speak to your twin? I wouldn't be here if it wasn't important." His tone was satirical with a darker edge.

Though he spoke to Cristaldo, his stare remained directed on me. I squirmed with discomfort that I tried desperately not to show. This was one man I didn't want to see or know any of my weaknesses. *What's his freakin' deal, anyway?*

"You've been holding out on me," Lucius said. "You've found one."

His words made no sense. "Found one? What do you mean by that?"

"She doesn't know?"

Cristaldo's expression darkened. "Nothing to know. She's here because her band, The Sirens, won a contest to play in Nero's."

"The Sirens. How perfectly delicious." The dark twin continued to stare at me, rattling my cage. "What instrument do you enjoy playing the most, Everly?"

He was not asking about music. I held on to my disgust, but glared at him.

"What do you want?" Cristaldo stepped between us, thankfully breaking up the vibe.

"We need you at the table. The House of Ribelle has asked for a sit-down in neutral territory. With the House of Anche."

"What, now?" Cristaldo barked.

"Yeah, now. If you can tear yourself away. Not sure I could. Maybe I should join in? Give you a hand taming this wild one?"

His creepy words made me realize I'd had enough.

I turned and tried to slip the key card into the slot on the door, my hands shaking while I struggled to hurry. *Damn.* The distinct sensation of the hounds of hell, nipping at my heels, focused my mind. On the second attempt, the device slipped into place. But the slight buzzing the lock emitted as the light switched from red to green drew their attention. I slammed the door shut in their surprised faces before they could react, thankful for the lock clicking soundly as it closed. I added the security chain for good measure, then slumped down onto the floor, my knees finally giving out. *What just happened?*

Chapter Seven

Cristaldo

"That was uncalled for." I glared at Lucius, letting him know his actions had riled me. He had the grace to look away at my warning.

"The Ribelle dogs are here and they already know about her. Where has she been hiding?"

"Some obscure town up in Canada."

"Explains why she's never been on anyone's radar before. So, much more importantly, have you fucked her yet?"

"Christ, Lucius, watch your tongue. Everly's my Forever Mate."

"The hell?" Lucius swallowed and quickly recovered. "You mean *our* Forever Mate."

"No, that's *not* going to happen. I'm setting limits. Right here and now. We might have had the same women in the past, but that stops with Everly. We'll leave that experience for Alessandro and Maximus."

The twins had never made it a secret that they wanted the same Forever Mate to share.

"It's like that, is it?" His eyes glittered with an unreadable emotion, but he gave a nod of acceptance. *There can only be one alpha, twins or not.*

"It's exactly like that. Hands off if you want to keep them."

"Not sure the House of Ribelle feels the same way."

"Why? What are they asking about?"

"Not sure I should answer that when you're acting all alpha male. You might blow a gasket." He pursed his lips, punching the button to direct the elevator we entered.

"Tell me. Now."

"Fine. They're challenging the right of the House of Luceres to keep her under their roof. She might be capable of being one of theirs — a dual breed. Or worse yet, only of their lineage. You know that, right? Until testing is concluded, we can't be certain. All we can know so far — judging from your response — is that she has the gene to become one of us."

My beast howled and I worked hard to stop him from going for his throat. "She's of our lineage and stays with me. If they think they can challenge me, they'll pay the price."

"That bad, huh?"

A violent urge to grab her *now* and escape to the desert was nearly impossible to resist. I wanted to hide us away. To keep her safe and sound. *Protect her with my life.*

"If you want my advice —"

"I don't. And stop talking. I need time to think."

I didn't have to look at my twin to know he was glowering at me. The waves of anger radiating in the air around us were making molecules shimmer erratically. *His problem, not mine.*

We exited my private elevator deep under the bowels of the casino in complete silence, then stalked through the tunnels to the House of Anche's secret underground war room built for the Vegas packs to resolve disputes. Since the split between houses over a thousand years ago, there had been just three separate packs of wolves, and I intended to keep it that way. The Ribelle dogs were more trouble than they were worth, while the Anche provided a necessary balance.

I aggressively pushed open the glass doors to the Curia, a huge stone area that had been made at great expense to duplicate the one from ancient Rome, prepared to confront my Ribelle enemies, Thaddeus the alpha and Rocco the enforcer. A large contingent of Anche pack members were in attendance as well, seated on the sunken stone tiers, there to keep the peace. I settled my sights on the group of wolves gathered, addressing them.

"Welcome, my fellow Senatores, to the House of Luceres." We were all descended from ancient Roman royalty, after all. Though charm might have soothed the savage beasts in fairy tales, the ones that sat in the war room stared at me with hunger and anticipation riding high in their eyes. Only fear was effective. And that could easily be arranged.

"Cristaldo," Thaddeus said, his mouth pinched. A deep frown marred his forehead, mirrored by his enforcer, Rocco, with whom I'd had the interesting altercation earlier. As soon as I got my hands on the idiot in charge of selling seats for the concerts and who'd sold two of Rocco's dogs tickets, causing the enforcer to rush in to check out the traitor's intel, I would put an end to that ever occurring again. By now, news of Everly's arrival had swept through Vegas quicker than a desert dust storm.

"Thaddeus." I stood tall, my legs planted wide apart, my arms folded over my chest, and waited.

"It's come to our attention that a possible royal mate for our House of Ribelle has arrived."

"She's for the House of Luceres," I interrupted.

"How can you know that so soon? Has she been fully tested? DNA sequencing's a delicate process and takes time. And if the markers point to a possible dual affiliation to both houses, you know the law. We challenge for her."

"I am aware. Anything else?"

Rocco snarled. Thaddeus gave him a sharp nod and he remained seated. But it was obvious he was barely constraining himself. *Bring it on, cur.*

"You'll excuse me if I say we will need proof of it. The lab reports. If you have already finished the sequencing because of your awareness of her existence *before* she arrived, then that will change things, of course. If everything points to the House of Luceres, that is, and *only* then."

I knew no such thing, but admitting it put Everly at risk. And that could never happen. The House of Ribelle only wanted Everly for mating purposes. Fertility had dwindled in all packs in recent decades at an alarming rate. Finding a fresh bloodline was hope beyond measure and a royal one beyond price. All the gold on Earth ever discovered or that would be found in the future was but a pittance to what she would be worth to our kind.

"We'll see you get your proof as soon as it can be arranged. Is there anything else?"

Rocco growled low in his chest at my dismissal. I leveled a steady glare his way, prepared to fight right now if necessary. The challenge was strong, and he began to shift, though it was forbidden in this neutral location, his eyes burning incandescent and his hands turning to claws. He was caught halfway between our world and the next. A damn uncomfortable situation, as I knew from firsthand experience, though the dog was weak to let it happen in this arena, the Curia, where it was prohibited. His infraction drew instant censure from Leonardo, alpha of the House of Anche.

"Stand down, Rocco—you know the punishment if you break the rules. Same as Cristaldo knows if he doesn't share his findings with everyone at his earliest convenience."

Leonard was a smart wolf, letting me know in the proper way that he expected the lab results as soon as possible.

The two wolves from the House of Ribelle got to their feet to strut away, needing to pass me on their way out. Thaddeus just nodded when he swept by, but Rocco stopped right in front of me, his stance confrontational. "I don't trust you, Cristaldo. If your lab reports look doctored in anyway, we will insist on doing our own. We have that right."

It was my turn to emit a deep rumble of warning.

Thaddeus turned at the doorway. "Rocco. Cristaldo knows the punishment for falsifying such reports, for obscuring the genetics of a potential mate. No need to say any more."

I did know. *Pit fight.* This female was worth taking the ultimate challenge for, if her bloodlines pointed to the rarest of events—coming before or during the split when Romulus and Remus' differences had created the warring factions — that she carried both their heritages. If so, she could be mated to *either* house.

Not going to happen. I'd see her mated to me and kept away from the Ribelle at all costs, claim her before they could. But the waiting, the need to know if my claiming her would harm her in anyway, was driving me insane. My wolf wanted to rush to her now. Though I could make her a she-wolf with my bite alone, as could any werewolf, it was a dangerous enterprise. Many had died during the transition. It went best when DNA matched to an ancient lineage of wolves.

Lucius and I made our way back through the tunnels, and when he deemed it safe, my twin spoke. "Christ, bro, that was a really bad idea. What are we going to do?"

"She's my mate. I just need to hurry the proof." She was going to be mine no matter *what* I had to do.

"But the dates will be wrong. You suggested there was a DNA sequencing called *before* she arrived."

"No need to parrot my words. I was there, damn it!" *What a clusterfuck.* "I have to go." I strode down the hallway and away from Lucius.

"You be careful, bro. This situation could cause an all-out war, break the truce we've all worked so hard to maintain for so long. Do you want to go back to that? Remember Helen of Troy and that fucking mess," he called after me.

"This female's worth it," I countered over my shoulder.

"Maybe, but watch your back. Things could go bad fast. There's a blood moon coming."

I entered the elevator without answering and hit the number that would take me back to Everly's room. The urge to smooth things over with her was my first priority.

I knocked louder on her door than I intended, blood pumping through me. My instincts had been ratcheted up to highest alert by the meeting with the House of Ribelle. A sense of sand running out of the hourglass ate at me, igniting flames of unease that swept through my body.

When the door slowly opened, revealing Everly, I kept myself from leaping on her and dragging her away with me with the greatest of difficulty.

I held on to the doorframe and gazed at the vision she made, with her hair floating around her shoulders and her face devoid of the makeup that she didn't need to look gorgeous. Dressed in a T-shirt, jeans and a hoodie, she looked beautiful beyond compare.

"I came to check on you. To apologize for my brother's rudeness."

She gave me a discerning look, her crystal green eyes bottomless pools of wisdom.

"You two are nothing alike, other than in outward appearance. Even then, I could tell you apart *anywhere*."

Her words inspired and comforted at the same time. Being mistaken for Lucius happened all too often, and having his exploits added to my growing legend was not beneficial now that *she* was here. *Only to having others fear me.*

"I take it he was too busy to apologize in person?" she asked, her voice crisped by sarcasm.

"It's not in him. He's always had his own way."

"Is it in you?"

"What?"

"To say you're sorry if you've made a mistake or been rude?" She clearly wanted to know the answer.

She stood her ground, looking up at me through those thick black eyelashes fanning her doe-like eyes. She pulled her hoodie tighter, outlining delicious curves and drawing my full attention.

"Never had to do so before," I ventured.

"And now?" She wasn't going to let it go. It was one of those defining moments and it made my gut churn uncomfortably. No male, let alone female, had ever talked this way to me. I would have shut them down in a second.

"My mother once said that anyone can learn something new with six weeks' practice," I said in a lighter tone. My words surprised me, but the memory of how happy my mother had made my father burned in my mind. She'd been a female alpha to his. So rare, it defied logic.

"Nice sidestep, *Wolfie*."

"I've taken women over my lap and given them a good spanking for less cheek, *la mia bella ragazza dolce*." My wolf demanded that I take her now.

Her skin flushed and her arresting, oh-so-womanly fragrance grew stronger, singeing the air. I drew a deeper breath into my starved lungs, making her eyes widen farther. Then I remembered that was exactly what had pissed her off about my twin.

"Sorry, but your scent is amazing." I realized belatedly what I had admitted to.

"So, you can say it," she teased. I wanted to take her over my knee, pull down her panties and teach her who was boss. But my need to keep myself in check mattered more...even though I was holding on to my control by one very, very thin thread that could stretch to breaking point at any second. But the shift between us was welcome — she looked less defensive now. I let go of the doorframe and advanced into the room.

"Apparently so," I quipped. Never had a female interested me more.

She didn't back up and I took it as a good sign.

"I'm going to need you to take a knee and make a solemn vow."

"What the heck are you talking about?" Eyes blazing, she stood her ground.

"I need your promise that word of my apology *never* leaves this room. Under penalty of a severe spanking."

"That's not going to happen." She continued to hold her ground, though her lips quivered. The idea aroused her even though a frown popped up, marring the space between her eyebrows. "What did your brother mean by your having found one?"

Damn Lucius, for letting that slip. "He meant finding such an intriguing female to spend time with."

She narrowed her eyes. "I don't believe you. You're hiding something from me."

"And you're not hiding anything from me? Does the name Jason Stubbs ring a bell?"

My misdirection worked. Her fair skin flooded with color. My mouth watered, imagining how hot her body would feel under mine, all flushed and glowing with desire for me.

"That's none of your concern." She glared, her body rigid. *Jason Stubbs better not show his face anywhere near me. He'll be a dead man.*

"It is if the Satan's Devils are going to descend on my place of business and cause an issue." The idea was laughable.

"Oh, I hadn't thought of that. Have I put your people in danger? I'm sorry if I have." Her look of concern for others gave me pause.

"I assure you, all my people are well-trained. I will personally see to it he never bothers you again."

"What does that even mean?"

"Enough about him." I dismissed the idea and moved one step closer.

"I have to go to bed soon, so you need to leave."

She licked her lips, the tiny pink point of her tongue slipping out and washing over their plushness. The action sparked the lust in me, pushing me to the edge.

"You enjoyed our kiss. You want this. I defy you to say differently," I said, taunting her. The sweet, musky scent of her arousal proved it. I was that close to taking her without permission. One tiny movement, one tiny whimper from her and I would slip into the void, control gone.

"I can't...I don't know why...why I want you so badly. You're an egotistical bastard—"

All I heard was that she wanted me.

I closed the distance between us in a flash, then crushed her to my chest and took her mouth. She softened against my lips and my lust incinerated. I had to have her. My inner wolf roared with power, demanding to be released. I picked her up and threw her over my shoulder then stalked from the room, hellbent on getting her to my lair.

Chapter Eight

Everly

"Let me down!" I pounded on Cristaldo's back in the elevator, incensed that he'd had the bloody gall to pick me up like some kind of caveman and haul me away.

Instead of answering, he swatted me in the butt, making me even angrier. I couldn't see anything but his legs from my undignified position.

"Ouch. Stop that!"

Instead, he gave me a second and harder slap on my ass that brought heat to my loins and tears to my eyes. Biting my lips, I only managed to keep myself from hurling some salty language at him with the greatest of difficulty.

"I'm taking you with me to keep you safe."

"What do you mean? Has there been some kind of threat against me?" My heart stuttered at the idea.

The elevator stopped. He stepped out, and from my upside-down position I could see a rounded glass partition wall. It had built-in images floating in the glass, stunning even from my skewed angle of vision. A pack of timber wolves emerging from a forest stalked for a good twenty feet along the structure. They were so well-crafted by the unknown artist that I expected them to leap from the wall and attack. For a second, I actually forgot my dire situation.

"Who loves the wolves?"

"We all love wolves. What about you? Do you ever experience a longing to throw off the shackles of modern civilization and run naked?" His voice darkened and I shivered. I could well imagine him watching me running naked, looking to take me down, his breath hot on my neck.

"Ah, sometimes I wonder what it would be like to run through the forest, but I'd prefer to do it on my own two feet, not on paws. And definitely *not* naked." I was lying about the naked bit—I loved having no clothes on—but I forgave myself instantly. Wolfie did not require any encouragement from me.

The space in front of us opened up quite abruptly. I had a vision of blurred legs and feet as they swept by me in a flash.

"Help me!" I shouted at them. Surely someone would stop this?

"She's fine. I've got this. It's just cosplay," he said, his tone filled with shades of mirth. He swatted me again as if to prove his good intentions.

"No. It's not! And you can see we're not in costume," I countered. But it was too late—we were alone. Maybe I hadn't protested enough? I had to admit, being brought up here like this kind of affected me on a level I hadn't experienced before. Getting all lustful from dominance is normally not my thing.

He slammed the door closed with one foot and threw me down on a large sofa. I scrambled to sit up, wanting to regain the advantage. His eyes bored into mine with the intensity of a thousand suns. I licked my lips, unable to stop staring at him. He looked dangerous. *Predatory.* The very air seemed to shimmer around him. His eyes grew far more intense, changing color to a bright cobalt blue for one spit second, but it was gone so quickly that I wasn't certain if it had been my imagination. His long legs closed the distance between us in a heartbeat.

"Tell me what's going on?" My throat was dry and my words come out huskily. He sat and pulled me into his arms. At least he wasn't spanking me anymore. I shivered with the sensation of the memory of his large hands on me.

"We were so rudely interrupted earlier, *la mia bella donna.*"

"Don't call me that! Tell me what the hell is going on."

He ran the back of one hand down my cheek. "Like the finest silk. *Sei una donna così bella,*" he murmured. My skin erupted in goosebumps. His speaking Italian compliments in my ear worked all too well, if the expected results were my being turned on. Everything sounded that much sexier and more sensuous, spoken in the language of love.

"What's going on? I need explanations or I'm out of here." It was best to make him think I had control of this.

"You are denying what's going on between us. Why?" He actually seemed confused, like he'd never been turned down by a woman before. He probably hadn't, looking like he did with the riches of Midas tucked into his bank account. Casinos were cash cows.

"I'm not that kind of woman."

"No, but you are *all* woman," he purred, making me exhilarated and furious and turned on, all at once. My body was filled with so much emotion that my skin felt tight, like I was about to burst at the seams.

"Why deny ourselves the pleasure? Don't you believe in destiny? You are here, I am here. Just say the word and I will make all your dreams come true."

I pulled away, intending to jump to my feet, but his arms held me firmly in place.

"Let me go. Until you explain what's going on, no touching. Be warned, I come armed."

He shook his head, looking mystified. "What are you talking about?"

I unzipped my hoodie and showed him the six throwing knives I carried. Needing their security had made me strap them on tonight. I hadn't been wrong to think that way, not judging by recent developments.

He chuckled, shocking me. "Is that all?" Then his eyes narrowed. "Do they contain silver?"

"What? Why does that matter?" More mystified than angry now, I needed answers.

He shook his head. "You are full of surprises. Are you any good at throwing them?"

"Passable." I was darned good, but my mother hadn't raised a braggart.

"Show me."

I was glad to have something to do other than sit so close to a man who destroyed all my good sense. If I didn't know better, I'd swear that he'd discovered a pheromone that enticed women in. It wasn't as though he didn't have the money for the research and development of said item.

"What do you want me to hit?" I asked brightly. "Maybe we might want to go somewhere else? This is a rather nice office." All lush fabrics, gleaming glass and fresh greenery made me wish for my plywood throwing board. Black-and-white artwork along with what appeared to be a large family portrait filled an entire wall. Not to mention an amazing photograph that I recognized from having drooled over it online.

"Is that Peter Lik's *Phantom*? I love that image. So otherworldly and awe-inspiring."

"Indeed. Well, if you're accurate, try for the smug bastard on the left in the family painting, Great Uncle Veto. I never liked him — he wasn't good to Aunt Marie. But if you miss and hit one of the pricier Ansel Adams or the *Phantom*, I might be a bit perturbed."

I raised my eyebrows. "It's a rather expensive oil painting. Are you certain?"

He shrugged. "Easy enough to replace. I know the artist. He'd be happy to paint another in its place."

I hadn't thought about how his money must draw in so many kinds of people, but I needed to get this done. I swept my mind clean of everything else and moved into my throwing stance, pulling out a knife and grasping it in the hammer grip in preparation. The best knife throws avoided any spin and, well, hit their intended targets. I let the sucker fly, using a smooth thrust of my stiffened wrist long strengthened from countless hours of practice. It hit Great Uncle Veto dead center of his scowling face, right between the disapproving eyes.

Silence greeted my maneuver. I whirled around to see appreciation riding high in those creamy brown eyes. *Creamy? Get a grip.* But it was sweet not to have him just be thinking of jumping my bones for a minute. *Like you're not thinking the same way?*

"Nice. Can you do that every time?" he asked. He leaned back on the sofa, splaying his legs, and I couldn't help myself. I glanced at his package. *Oh my. Don't look.* It was far too obvious that he could back up all his boasts.

I shrugged, averting my eyes. I was going for nonchalance, though I could hear the slight tremor in my voice. Was it getting hot in here? "Pretty much. I practice lots. That's the secret no one wants to hear. And it does help with my drumming. Strengthens my wrists."

"You throw with both hands?" His eyebrows shot up. I enjoyed surprising him more than I could say. I was also enjoying this part of our interaction more than I should have. I seemed to keep forgetting who he was…a man used to taking what he wanted, and that we were all alone right now. Well, except for the servants that had to be somewhere around. But they must have been loyal only to him, by the way they'd ignored my entreaties to intervene earlier.

"Both hands? Yeah. Gift passed down from my father's side of the family."

"That's a useful ability we share." He seemed pleased. A smile even tugged at the corner of his mouth. Some of the knots in my stomach began to smooth out.

"You're ambidextrous?" I asked. It was a rare situation to be able to use each hand equally well and not just favor one hand over the other for certain tasks, and one I treasured as a drummer.

"Yes. We all are."

"All your relatives?"

The conundrum of several people having the rare ability took me away for a moment before I jerked myself back to what really mattered. "Yes."

"Okay, we need to talk. Has there been a threat against me? Is that why you brought me up here all cavemanlike? You can't just do that, you know? Billionaire or no billionaire. I have rights." At least his surreal actions made sense on some level, if he were worried about me. A part of me was rather flattered, if he'd brought me here to protect me from Jason Stubbs.

His expression darkened. "Come here," he said.

I sat back down again, as far away as the sofa allowed, and stiffened my spine. I needed to say this. "Is it my ex, Jason Stubbs? Because if it is, I'm sorry for your trouble. I never thought he'd carry things this far, all the way from Canada. I have him on record with the police for the things he's done, so I can have him arrested."

"You're sorry for it?" He frowned. "In what way would it be your fault?"

"I brought my troubles to your doorstep. I have such bad taste in men."

"This has happened before?" Anger rippled under the cool, handsome surface, though he remained perfectly still. Why could I read him so well? Or was I just deluding myself?

"No. Well, kind of." Did the guy who had attached himself to me in elementary school count? I shook my head, not wanting him to think I was a complete idiot. "Jason was the first man I've really been with. He was so charming at first, took such an interest in me, I thought he might be — an okay guy to date." I almost said 'the one', but that sounded too lame to share. I did have a belief in there being only one exact perfect mate for me. *Somewhere*. Whether I found him in this lifetime was the part up for grabs.

"Never blame yourself for others' actions. I'm certain he just saw the specialness in you and wanted to be part of it." He nodded once.

He thinks I'm special? A smile must have formed on my lips, because I found him staring right at me when I glanced over. I swallowed hard, trying not to move.

Suddenly, he was closer. Heat thrummed under the taut surface of my skin and hunger rose from deep inside me, a hunger that overcame all reservations, all sanity. When I looked into those beautiful brown eyes, I fell. Fell into him, needing his touch as I'd never needed anything before. So much power filled his hard body that I reeled from the sheer intensity. *See. Me.* The words fired across my heated brain.

When he leaned forward and pulled me into his arms, I put up little resistance. A mewling sound filled my ears. Then his lips descended and claimed mine. His scent surrounded me. *Cocooned* me. There was only this exact moment, when his plush, oh-so-warm lips pressed against mine, forcing me to surrender. *Everything*. I opened my mouth and let him inside to plunder the depths. Then he backed off and pulled my tongue into his mouth, before sliding back inside me, over and over, until I was dizzy with lust. The room spinning, I spoke the words of no return.

"Make love to me."

He groaned, then picked me up and swung me over onto him as though I weighed nothing. I was held so tightly against him now that his erect cock pressed against my pussy. Heat fired in me to tug him even closer, to pull him inside my body, to relieve the ache that threatened to burn me. I ground against him, unable to control myself. Dimly, I was aware that this couldn't possibly be real. To feel this much desire to be with another? To mate? It was pure insanity. But it sucked me in even as I questioned it, even as I understood I should resist. My willpower had vanished.

"I will pleasure you and never, never let you go, my special one. I've waited for so long for you. Give me everything. I *own* you. You are mine."

His words took time to register. But when they did, I was unable to breathe, the air frozen in my lungs.

"No! I can't! I can't do this again." I struggled helplessly at his chest. It was like pushing at an immovable stone. He continued to cover my face and chest with kisses, sucking a nipple into his mouth through my thin T-shirt and nipping down on it, sending powerful waves of pleasure all through my body. "Stop it! I don't want to do this!" I began to hit him with my clenched fists.

This time it registered. He froze as well, then pulled back from me and pushed my hair away from my blazing face with both hands. He held my face still between them, his touch gentler now.

"What's wrong? I thought you wanted this?" His voice was throaty, as though he'd overused it. His confusion was the only thing keeping me from biting or scratching at him to let me go. I had led him on.

"I can't be here. Do this. Let you think that you own me. *No one* owns me."

He remained silent and the seconds ticked by. I watched him working hard to gather himself. I had cost him—his ego and vanity were suffering, but he stayed his lust. If he felt anything like the way I did, it took all he had, and then some. He helped me to my feet.

"I want you to meet someone who will see to your needs while you are here."

I nodded.

A moment later the door burst open and in swept a man of indeterminable age with extra-high hair, intense blue eyes and a well-fitting midnight-blue suit with a fragrant red rose pinned to his lapel. His expression was animated and kindly.

"Everly Affini, welcome to the Glitter Palace! I'm Sly, majordomo of the House of Luceres. May I say how *very* pleased we are to have you stay with us. You were *so* good in concert last night." He gestured as he welcomed me aboard, making him all the more endearing to me. He reminded me of one of my great-uncles back home when he took my hand and kissed the back of it in an elaborate old-country gesture.

"Thanks. I appreciate that."

"Anything you need, call me, day or night. I'm a light sleeper. Would you like me to see to your bag?"

"I'll take care of it, thank you, Sly," Cristaldo said.

"Of course, sire." He bowed once and backed out of the room, leaving us alone again.

"Why does everyone call you sire?" I asked. Having met Sly made me feel better, or less agitated, at being out of my element with no friends to call upon. I'd always counted on friends.

He gave me a look. "Just tradition in the House of Luceres. Why? Does it bother you?"

I shrugged. "Just different."

"Come. I'll show you to your room."

Chapter Nine

Cristaldo

My body vibrated with the agonizing pressure of not claiming her. Never had I wanted a female more. *Everly.* Her very name spoke to me on levels that I had never known existed. Frustrated as I was with my immediate need to have her or hit the wall with my fists, I could still appreciate her courage and honesty. Damn that asshole who'd tormented her and sent her to me unable to give herself what she most needed. *What I can give her. Everything her heart desires.*

The fragrance of her lust, the feel of her curvy little body, the soft spot where she'd whimpered when I'd kissed her neck...*everything* about her filled up my senses. The urge to keep her close was growing by leaps and bounds. A clock ticked louder in my brain. How long would I have control over myself? My brief run in the desert had not been near enough to release all the pent-up frustration that threatened my immortal soul.

I stopped at the doorway to the suite I'd chosen for my mate. I would keep her safe in this gilded cage, but would she forgive me for not sharing the truth of who was behind these threats? Thoughts of my sister hardened me. Yes, it was worth it. Some day she would understand.

Opening the door, I waved away the hovering servants who had prepared the room for Everly. Their withdrawal revealed a bank of curved floor-to-ceiling windows framing the spectacular light show that was Vegas at midnight, the witching hour, and it made Everly gasp aloud.

"What a magnificent view," she murmured, following me inside. She stood and stared out at the night sky, and I clenched my hands in tight fists, to keep from taking her. A bed was close, the floor was even closer and the temptation was too great to stay.

"Let me know if you need anything." *Claim her*, my wolf howled, struggling to take me over. Lust hung on a knife's edge, threatening to consume me. *Us.*

"This is far more than I need. I thought you'd chose another room in the hotel and keep the location secret?"

"I protect my own."

She frowned, then seemed to think better of arguing.

"Keep the door locked at all times. Don't let anyone in unless you know them, like Sly."

"What about you?" Her tone was light and I realized she was flirting with me.

"*Especially* me. The coming blood moon is what's responsible for all these rising infernal passions this week. Don't worry, this will pass." I wanted to reassure her. Though once we started our mating, I couldn't imagine the passion and lust I felt for her easing. I would have her in every way, fill her with my essence until no other wolf would come within fifty feet of her and not know I had claimed her for my own. This intense drive to know every inch of her body was becoming too strong. I should run tonight, but my need to protect her was stronger.

"Blood moon? Right. I've heard about that. A super blood wolf moon is due in a few days and is supposed to be spectacular. Wow! And I couldn't have a better view to enjoy it!"

Her innocence only made my urges all the more difficult. I forced my feet to move, to take me away from the temptation to do what I wanted more than my life at the moment.

"Keep your door locked," I repeated.

I stared at the closed door after Cristaldo had left. Had any woman ever experienced such an overwhelming urge to throw herself at a man she hardly knew? So much power filled his hard body, with those broad shoulders, that tapering waist and the lean, muscular abs I sensed had to be under that expensive clothing. He was the epitome of a wolf in sheep's clothing, his designer suit a smokescreen. It was obvious by the way he walked, talked and flashed his virile power — an alpha male in prime, peak condition, his body built for endurance. He would make love like a champion, I had no doubt. The vision of our being with each other, sharing our bodies, made my knees weaken to water.

Why deny yourself? My mind focused on the obvious. *You only have a few days together. This time will never come again.* But something was stopping me from acting on it. Perhaps the intuition that I would not walk away from an encounter with Cristaldo entirely whole.

My stomach grumbled from hunger, but I ignored it. I prowled around the room, too hyped to go to bed. The room was lavish, over-the-top luxury. Most women would have soaked in its splendor, but I had the intense urge to go out into the forest, to walk on rich earth and green moss, to fill my lungs with nature's fragrance. Fishing trips with my father came to mind. Alone time with him once a year, camping for a few precious days, had been the highlight of my summer. Freshly caught pickerel, fried in sweet butter over an open fire pit, was food for the gods. My mouth watered at the memory.

Thinking about it was only making me hungrier. I sat in a chair and stared out at the awesome view of Vegas. Why had he told me not to let even him in? He wanted me. That was obvious. He was being a gentleman, letting me decide! *Of course. Crap.* I was confused.

I got up and went to the wet bar. *Hmm. What to have?* I poured myself a tumbler of X-rated pink vodka made from blood oranges, mango and passion fruit, plunked myself back down again in one of the comfy easy chairs and took a long swig of one of my favorite drinks. The only thing missing was my friends. *Holy crap.* I'd forgotten to check in.

I yanked my phone out of my pocket and hit the button for Cleo's number.

"Everly. Is everything okay?"

I swore at myself for taking so long to reassure my bandmates when I heard the concern in her voice. "I'm so sorry. Time just got away from me. I'm fine. I'm upstairs in the penthouse suite with the door locked." *Or at least it will be soon as I get around to it.* Guilt made me stalk over to the door to engage the lock as we chatted.

"Wow, he's really taken you under his wing," Cleo said. "What did he say about Jason? Was he behind the threats?"

"Yeah, looks like it." It was then I realized he hadn't *exactly* said it was Jason, but it must have been. Cristaldo hadn't denied it.

"That *bastard*. I wonder if he came alone or brought some fellow club members with him?"

"I don't know all the details. God, I hope not." Embarrassment washed over me at being the catalyst for such deplorable actions. "I'll ask in the morning."

"So, you're up there with the gorgeous Cristaldo." She drawled out the words.

"Nothing happened. Just a kiss is all."

"A kiss is *not* nothing, girlfriend. It's a beginning. Damn, I knew it. I'm going to win this bet. You'd better be saving up all your money to buy me that magnum of champagne."

There were several bottles of bubbly lined up in the over-sized bar fridge not twenty feet away. Maybe it wouldn't cost me a thing? Then I startled. What was I turning into? I'd buy it myself. It made me more determined than ever now to win the bet and add another Howling Wolf to my collection. "A magnum, is it? That's a bit steep."

"So, you know you're going to lose," she crowed.

"I know no such thing! When I asked him to stop, he did just that."

"Ha! I can tell by your voice that you found that difficult. God, how did you *not* jump his bones? He's so damn hot."

"Okay, enough about men. Call me in the morning, okay? Soon as you're ready. I want to get out of this place. See Vegas while we're here." My skin itched with the need to break free of invisible bonds.

"Is that wise? You know, with what's going on?"

"Damn that man." I wasn't sure which man I meant at that moment. Both were keeping me from what I wanted. *To be free. To be myself.*

"Maybe Cristaldo will supply bodyguards? He seems to have a lot of them around."

"I'll ask. Hopefully it won't be too expensive." I was always on a tight budget, between helping my parents for free in our restaurant and saving to promote The Sirens.

"Okay, talk tomorrow. Oh, and don't do anything I wouldn't do. Which leaves lots up for grabs. Just sayin'."

"No intention of it."

I hung up, laid my phone on a bedside table and swallowed half of my drink. Chatting with Cleo had helped. I tugged off my tennis shoes and jeans, then placed them neatly in the closet, which was when I discovered racks full of clothes, pretty much all in my size. I ran my hand over the sumptuous fabric of the couture chic that made my attempts at fashion look pathetic in comparison. Ignoring the temptation, I closed the closet door then padded over to the bed. I'd sleep in my T-shirt.

I pulled back the beautiful covers of white-on-white brocade on the king-sized bed and crawled into the lap of luxury to lie back against a nest of soft pillows and stare at the Sistine Chapel ceiling. *Awesome.* I picked up my drink and finished the last of it. The alcohol flooded my system, warming my body and making me acutely aware that my center still ached with need.

Damn it. My clothes were suffocating me. I tore off my tee, enjoying freeing my breasts to the air, then pulled down my panties and tossed them onto the floor. Naked was so much better. I'd never been ashamed of my body. Sometimes I even drummed for hours in the nude. I found great freedom in throwing away inhibitions.

I slipped my hands down to my breasts, enjoying the weight and fullness. I ran my fingers around the tips, the nipples hardening instantly, then tugged on the sensitive nubs, making myself moan.

The urgent need for release made me spread my legs wider, exposing myself. I closed my eyes and thought of Cristaldo's hands on my breasts. His lips on my nipples. His cock hard and pushing against my slick folds. His voice in my ear.

'I need you to do everything a woman does for her man,' he instructed me. *'Do that and I will give you more pleasure than you've ever dreamed of. Can you do that?'*

I nodded, panting. "Yes."

Then he was entering me with all his hugeness. *Stretching me, filling me.*

I reached down and pushed aside the soft outer lips, gaining access to my clit. It throbbed, and I circled it with my fingers, then tugged at it, the swollen nub pulsating with pleasure.

"Take me. Harder." My voice and body were swept along as I rubbed faster. I pushed two fingers deep inside and thrust in and out at a tempo that made the entire world drop away. I was close. *So close.* My body wanted to drop over the precipice, to release itself from the throes of a primal need.

He thrust into me while his hands grasped my hips, pulling me up against him, his balls pressed tight against my ass when his body locked into mine. He was so huge. So hard. Almost unable to take the violation, I moaned as unbelievable pleasure streaked through me...and I was greedy for more.

'That's it, take it all. Let me in, la mia bella donna. I want all of you. Let me do this – fill you with all of me.' His words pierced me. So real – it was as if he were inside me, speaking right now. His voice thrummed through me. Electrified, I let it happen, let him take control of my body and mind. It was beyond exhilarating, this strange new sensation. It was everything that I never knew I wanted. *Never knew existed. Until now.*

'I claim you, bella. I will never hurt you. Let me share all that we are, to allow us to answer the call of the wild. Our bodies and minds and hearts as one, locked together, unable to pull apart. I will take you beyond anything you could ever imagine. Let your body feel the pleasure of binding. Come for me.'

"Yes!" The waves crested and my body convulsed with an orgasm that went on and on. Heat and juices mingled in the air, the electrifying aroma of sex.

* * * *

I stroked down the thick length of my cock as I controlled her in my mind with the power of suggestion. A rare telepathic link between us allowed me to be with her in the moment. *To feel what she feels, see what she sees, able to respond to her every need. Her every desire, her every wish is mine to fulfill.* The intensity of shared sensation drove me to push her to the limit, to make her feel *everything* I possessed. With my lust to claim her, I bent her to my iron will. My cock filled her and locked within her receptive body, pushing us to become one.

She moved with me as if we'd always been together, each touch electrified, looking at me with those Bambi eyes. I whispered my intentions, my need to have her open all the way for me. To let me inside her body and soul. Our bodies were perfect for each other, meant to be.

When I came, I was inside her, her luscious pink center tightening around me. My cock pulsed in ecstasy and an untamable howl escaped my throat.

Chapter Ten

Everly

I'm running, listening for pursuit. A slight sound makes my ears twitch back. He's not far behind me. I haven't been able to outrun him, try as I might. My heart pounds, thudding in my eardrums. I leap across a narrow stream, the ancient waterway an easy jump. I land on all four limbs, then turn right to follow the hidden path to the spot we love so much. On one side of me looms a steep rockface, on the other a meandering brook. The waterfall appears around a bend, flowing down into a pool. Beside its magnificence, the open mouth of a cave beckons.

He catches up and nips playfully at my side. His eyes are bright blue, his fur tan and luscious, fragrant with nature's scent of wind and sun. We tussle in greeting, his paws working to take me to the ground. I resist him. A howl rents the air.

The image shattered. I'd dreamed of being a wolf before and found it disturbing. This time, it had been better, more natural. I opened my eyes and looked at the unfamiliar setting. Then I remembered where I was, what had happened the night before, and my body overheated with the memory.

Crap. What is going on with me?

I leapt out of bed and rushed to the bathroom to shower. I stood under the harsh stream of the coldest setting for long minutes, wanting to rid myself of whatever nonsense seemed to have claimed me. *Maybe it was a fever dream?* Nothing had made sense since I'd entered this penthouse. *Heck, since I came to Vegas, for that matter.* I leaned one hand against the cold tile of the huge shower, bracing myself. Finally shivering with cold, I turned the setting to warm to shampoo my hair and wash myself before getting out.

Better. I surveyed myself in the mirror while I wrapped a huge fluffy bath towel around my body and another around my soaking wet hair. I looked good, my eyes huge and greener than normal, hiding surprisingly well the sensual thoughts I'd been having and acting on. *Ahh.* But I had enjoyed it too, no denying that — just thinking about it turned me on. *Mind out of the gutter, Everly.*

I quickly dried off and combed out my hair before using the blow dryer I discovered in a drawer. Day two of our grand adventure and the outside world screamed at me to join in the fun.

Resolving to keep myself too busy to dwell on the events of the night before, I realized that if I wanted clean clothes, I'd have to wear something from the closet. *Has anyone worn them before me?* No. The tags were still on them! Choosing a nice floaty sundress — Vegas was hotter than Hades in the summer — I also found clean underwear and slipped into them. I borrowed a pair of ballet flats in a matching hue to the cream-colored dress then tucked the knives away in a drawer. *For now.*

Satisfied that I was prepared to greet my host or that majordomo guy, Sly, I unlocked the door and ventured outside my room, hoping *someone* could point the way to a cup of coffee and some breakfast. No food after the concert had left me starving, though there had been lots of choices in the icebox that I could have consumed.

"Good morning, Miss Affini!" Sly greeted me in the hallway, rushing up as soon as I appeared. His suit was now a deep turquoise with a fresh white rosebud in the label. "I trust you slept well?" He leaned in and kissed me on both cheeks. *Right. Old-world.* Just his presence exuded a sense of normalcy that I was sorely in need of in my present circumstances.

"I did, as it happens." *Nightmares and sexual thoughts aside.* There was no point in complaining. I wasn't out on the street or being bothered by Jason Stubbs.

"And now you would be hungry. Correct? For a nice hearty breakfast?"

"You guessed correctly. Something about the desert makes me hungrier."

"Yes, the desert can bring out our appetites. I never feel more alive than when I'm here."

"Have you been Cristaldo's majordomo for long?"

He nodded with a smile. "Yes, more than a decade. I do so enjoy my job, seeing to his needs and the needs of his entire household."

"How many people work in the penthouse?" Curiosity filled me to discover more about how the other less-than-one percent of the world lived.

"Forty all told, on different shifts. Of course, that includes his limo drivers."

"Really? That's a lot of help for just one man," I mused.

"People enjoy working for him. He's a good boss who finds it hard to turn down anyone wanting work."

We fell in step and rounded one curved hallway, nearly bumping into Cristaldo striding toward us. Shyness after him having starred so prominently in my delicious late-night fantasy overcame me and I found it hard to look directly at him. When I finally chanced it, his eyes bore into my own with a directness that stunned me. *That burns.* I rubbed my thighs together in aggravation. *No. Not. Again.*

"Morning, *la mia bella donna*. Morning, Sly," he said. His lips quirked into a smug smile. Did he know what I had done last night? What I wanted to do right now?

"Morning, sire. I'll leave you to enjoy your meal." Sly left with a graceful wave of his hand. The guy was easy to like. I hoped more of the staff were as friendly once I got to know them. Then I was brought up short with the realization that that wasn't likely, since I'd be going home soon.

"Morning," I said. "I like it." I returned his smug smile.

"What's that?"

"The term beautiful."

"That's what you are." He nodded with satisfaction. He was dressed once more in expensive Armani, his suit only different in the slight sheen in the fabric, the subtle change of tie. His snowy shirt was fastened with heavy gold cufflinks and embedded with diamonds and gleamed in the morning light.

"You wouldn't be able to point me in the direction of a cup of coffee? I'm dying for one." *Almost as much as I'm dying to jump your bones.*

"We can't have that. Did you sleep well? Was the bed to your satisfaction?"

My skin prickled with goosebumps. Did he suspect? Had he heard me? Dear Lord, what was the deal with this place? How could I be expected to handle any more of this torture? *Insanity.*

"The bed was fine." I began to chew on a fingernail, something I hadn't done in years.

He took mercy on me and nodded. "Follow me."

I did, down another long curving hallway until the scent of coffee greeted my nose. I breathed in deeply, increasing my pace. Cristaldo led me into a nook that contained not only the promised coffee, but a choice of breakfasts. Trays of pastries, covered dishes that steamed around the edges and a hot beverage bar all greeted my hungry stare. His staff had been busy.

I pounced on the coffee pot, filling a giant mug with the essential brew and adding a liberal dash of thick cream. I drank it down standing there, that grabbed a plate and piled it high with strips of crispy bacon, fluffy scrambled eggs, pancakes and syrup. Ignoring my host, I perched on the first available chair and attached the food. Never had I been so famished. Politeness flew out of the window as I kept my focus on having my fill, trying to assuage something deep inside me that pinched and snarled with urgency.

When I had devoured every last morsel on my plate, I gulped down a second cup of coffee, then dabbed at my lips with a white linen napkin.

"Better?" Cristaldo asked, quirking an eyebrow.

"Much." I remembered my manners. Damn, now that one need was satiated, another was demanding attention. *Again.* "Thank you. Now, about the situation. I can't sit around this hotel all day waiting to play."

"Who said anything about your playing again?" His face glowered while his words stunned.

In an instant, all the air was sucked right out of the room. "What do you mean? *Of course*, I'm playing. That's why I'm here—why we're all here." *The bloody nerve. Suggesting I'm too frightened to go out on stage just because that idiot Jason showed up.*

His voice thundered, though his expression remained shut down. "I will keep you safe. Here. With me."

"You can't expect me to stay cooped up here with you. I'm not your prisoner!" I stood, hands on hips, defiant and ready to fight. Who did he think he was?

His expression turned to coldest granite. "The threats against you are credible. You were nearly attacked last night. I won't have that happen again."

"Doesn't this place have bodyguards? I'll hire some. I want to see this town while we're here. Not hide away like a scared mouse. Or go home with my tail tucked between my legs." I shook my head vehemently. "That's *not* who I am."

Our eyes locked in mortal combat. He remained silent and I pressed my advantage. "I'm not an idiot. I'll take precautions. Jason Stubbs will not be a problem. Besides, he's *my* problem. I'll go to the police and show them the restraining order I filed in Canada. Maybe they can pick him up for following me here?"

"I will guard you. Stay away from the police. They will only complicate things."

"No, *absolutely* not. You have other things to do. You run a casino, for heaven's sake." The thought of being with him twenty-four-seven scared me right to the core. How could I control myself if he were always in my presence? I'd surely break under the strain and end up throwing myself at him and embarrassing myself.

"I will make the time. End of discussion, if you want to play with your band tonight." His tone was final, edged with steel.

I didn't want to go home or let my bandmates down. The compromise, though not perfect, was better than nothing. "Fine." I realized how ungrateful I must sound. "Thank you."

"You're welcome."

"I need to freshen up. Can I meet you at the elevators in five?"

He nodded. I raced back to my suite down the long, winding corridor that I somehow managed to navigate a second time and slammed the door behind me, my heart racing. I used the facilities and brushed my teeth, then pulled my hair up into a high ponytail that would keep it out of the way.

Five minutes later, right on the dot, I arrived at the elevator. Cristaldo was already standing there like a stern sentinel. I nodded and stepped inside the confining space, experiencing enough powerful testosterone on the ride down to make me clench and unclench my fists. *And other unmentionable parts.*

"What would you like to see?" he asked.

"Everything."

"Tall order, *bella*."

"Well, I'd like a chance to gamble a bit, though I know nothing about it. I mean, it's Vegas, right? I love the circus and all the rides, and the pirate show, of course. And a candied apple wouldn't go amiss. Oh, and see a concert. One of the headliners would be great."

"Easily arranged. Shall we go?"

I nodded and he held out his hand to me. When our fingers touched, the sparks of electricity jumped between us. I swallowed. *Oh boy*, this was going to be some day.

Walking down the Strip hand in hand with a billionaire was surreal. Cristaldo was all I was aware of. His warm body next to mine, his handsome face as he gifted me with the occasional smile — he appeared to be enjoying himself as well. And he was so casual about it, pointing out this and that as we stopped at different venues. I discovered I had to be careful, because each time I admired something, he bought it. In no time, the back seat of the chauffeured limo that followed us was filled with gifts.

The blast of the cannons enhanced the visual effects of the outdoor pirate show we stopped to watch, accompanied with the sharp odor of gunpowder, and sharing the experience with Cristaldo was priceless. But the ride on the Ferris wheel was the best of all. I imagined we were teenagers on a first date, though when I locked eyes with him, when we reached the lofty top that gave a spectacular view of the Strip, I saw no teenager, but a man with needs.

"What do you want out of life, Cristaldo?" It was an intimate question to ask with us sitting so close together and swaying gently in one of the colorful metal cars that made up the High Roller as though we were the only two people in the world, cradled away from the others and watching everything unfold below us. *Caught between two worlds.*

He shrugged. "The same as most people. To provide for my family and to make a good life."

"What does that life include for you?" I pressed.

He gently brushed the hair back from my forehead and gave me a look that dissolved me into a puddle of yearning.

"A wife and family. What about you? Do you want to marry?"

"I haven't given it much thought. I've been so busy trying to make a career in the music business. But yeah, one day I want to marry." Perched so high above everything and everyone, it all seemed possible. That maybe somehow, or someway, this could continue.

He nodded and smiled, squeezing my hand. "That's good. Life is too short to be alone."

I swallowed. "Yes, it is."

* * * *

"At this rate we'll have nothing left to see in Vegas by tomorrow noon," I joked as we strolled back toward the Glitter Palace, satiated from too much food and drink. Everything was so close in Vegas that we had walked most of the time, though his limousine had shadowed our every step.

"That's the plan." He grinned and I stilled. I disliked being thwarted, but seeing his beautiful smile was even harder to take. What would it be like to witness him being open and vulnerable all the time, like he'd been today? Hot desire pulsed through me, as thick as syrup in my veins.

The minefield that was Vegas had just gotten more explosive.

Chapter Eleven

Everly

Our evening concert began with high expectations, my bandmates primed to give the best show ever. I wanted that. For all of us. When the music began, I let it take over entirely, my breath rushing in and out in huge gasping gulps. At times my vision narrowed alarmingly, my performance beyond human understanding, beyond all reason, as passion threatened to burn me to cinders. I was used to the magic that overcame me as the beat flowed through me — but this — *this*? It was like playing with fire.

If last night's encore had been greeted with approval, tonight's enthusiasm gave me a sensation that we were rock stars descended from the gods. *Unbelievable. Exhilarating. Electrifying.*

When we took our final bow, holding hands, some of the crowd, already on its feet, became too frenzied, and a man rushed the stage.

Frozen in place, I looked around for my friends. The intruder jumped right in front of me, effectively blocking my path, but when the man launched himself at me a second later, a blur of movement intervened and I was shoved out of the way. I kept myself upright with great difficulty and missed some of the action. When I turned to see what had happened, the man who'd attacked me was on the floor, and Cristaldo was on top of him.

My protector's murderous expression would have put thunderclouds to shame. I half-expected to hear the bang of Thor's hammer off in the distance. More security members arrived and yanked the interloper to his feet then hauled him away, his outraged protests at his treatment turning the air blue.

Cristaldo swept me into his arms. "Are you all right?"

"I'm fine." His being there had stopped anything further from occurring and I was grateful.

"He could have hurt you. No more concerts for you." His voice fueled by anger, his words incensed me. He was right back to being all alpha after the amazing day we'd just spent together.

"But he didn't. Thank you. Shows how well-trained you and your team are. You should be proud. And it had to be a one-time thing. You'll see, tomorrow will be different. Just tell them to serve less alcohol or check on drug use. I'll bet that was the real culprit."

"It wasn't drugs or liquor. They wanted you, Everly." His low tone held a firmness of conviction that dismayed me. I pulled away from him.

"What on earth are you talking about? I'm just a drummer in a band."

He rubbed the back of his neck, closed his eyes and winced, like he was getting a really bad headache.

"Something wrong?" I asked.

"There's so much you don't know. That I can't share, not yet, much as I want to."

"What are you talking about? What don't I know?" His words sent unease slithering through me, though I was still angry.

"You'll have to trust me. It's for your own good."

I gave an unladylike snort.

"I think you do trust me. I think you know me better than you'll care to admit. We share an understanding."

His words only made me feel grumpier. I couldn't seem to find a neutral setting around this guy for the life of me. "I'm hungry and thirsty. When you're ready to have a proper conversation, call me. I don't beg. If it isn't freely given, it's not worth anything."

Cristaldo pursed his lips. *Fine. Be like that.*

I whirled around and joined my friends at the refreshment table. After reassuring them a few dozen times that I was fine, I checked out the fare provided to us. I had never been hungrier than I was in Vegas. I chugged a bottle of water then polished off a thick ham sandwich in a few bites. The meat was so good. Cleo gave me a look, her eyebrows rising in disbelief. She nibbled daintily on a cookie, her sweet tooth on display. She lived by the dessert-first rule. I grinned at her before slowing down my gluttony. *No more freakin' out my friends.*

"The dry desert does make one hungry for everything." Cristaldo was at my elbow, commenting, no doubt, on my table manners.

I narrowed my eyes. "Just for food." *Don't be getting any ideas, Wolfie.*

"Keep telling yourself that, if it helps."

I bit my lip to keep from firing back. I hated that I was so attracted to him, like I had no mind of my own. My body flooded with heat that I ignored. "I know my own mind."

"Do you? I see more than you know. You want me. But you're too scared to admit it."

I sputtered. "I'm not scared of anything. Least of all you!" I pointed a finger at his chest and he closed in tight, looming over me.

"Careful. I'll nip that errant finger and turn you over my knee to teach you some proper respect." His eyes glinted dangerously.

I wanted to go further with him. To feel his big hands pulling down my panties, exposing me to him, the heat of his breath tantalizing on my flesh. I swallowed. Oh yeah, some sweet fun that would be. *Crap.* I brought myself right back to the present with a sharp pinch on my arm.

He grinned at me, as if he knew what I was fantasizing. Hell, I was even certain I could detect the fragrance of my own arousal.

"You wouldn't dare," I said. *Yes, please take me in hand. Spank my bottom until it's nice and hot again, then let's kiss each other all over and make love until we can't move at all.*

New number one rule—don't challenge *Wolfie*, because the next thing he whispered in my ear suggested he had an inkling of what had happened last night in my suite. It had been so real, as if he'd really been inside my body. "You're not getting away with it tonight, *bella*."

I pretended I didn't have a clue what he was speaking about. "I'm not that kind of girl."

"Oh, I think you are, and a lot more. You want me, more than you are willing to say. We are the same, you and I. We both want to live life to the fullest. Can you deny it? This attraction for one another?"

Lucius rushed up to us, halting right in front of his brother and bringing our conversation to a screaming halt. "I need you right now, Cristaldo. We have a situation."

The deep rumble of Wolfie's breath was followed immediately by a frown. He was as turned on as me. I'd lay odds on that and win big. *Thank you, fate, for saving me.* The last thing I needed was a guy like that to turn my head, because he was right. It was more than physical attraction now. Our day together had proved it, which made it all the more difficult. It would take a month of Sundays to recover if this continued. But this had to end. We came from different worlds—a vast ocean existed between us.

After Cristaldo bestowed a quick kiss on my cheek, the twin brothers stalked off together. Serge, the guy who had been in charge of our concert from the beginning, came over.

"How are you doing, Everly?" he asked, his dark eyes appearing keen to know.

"Fine. What's going on?"

"How's that?"

"Cristaldo just hurried off with his brother. Everything okay?"

"There is a lot going on right now. It could be most anything." He shrugged. "From something here, to something happening in another one of their casinos."

"Other casinos?"

"Didn't you know? The family owns a chain of them all around the world. From Cancun, Macau, New

Jersey, Los Angeles, to Vancouver, Canada. They've done remarkably well indeed. They're billionaires *many* times over."

"No kidding." I suddenly felt way, *way* out of my league. What was a guy like that doing spending time with me?

My sails flattened. Obviously, I was just a plaything that had taken his attention for the moment. The guy had his pick of women, all around the world. I could just imagine how many would be more than ready to step up for the kind of fun and games I could only guess at, and he most likely expected. In comparison to that, what was a little spanking? Just a tidbit before the main course.

Serge must have caught my change in mood, because he turned thoughtful, rubbing his chin. "I should also say, we're not all about the money. Most of us have worked hard to earn it, and we don't think it makes us any better than anyone else."

"You share in the wealth?"

"We all do. It's pack money." He startled, like he'd given out too much intel.

"Pack? Why do you call it pack money?" I had never heard the expression before.

He looked decidedly uncomfortable now. "No real reason." He rubbed harder at his chin. "But what I mean is that the money doesn't put them into a different stratosphere. Everyone in the extended family works for their living—at all kinds of jobs, whatever they're best suited for or have a wish to learn. In fact, the other twin brothers of the House of Luceres, Alessandro and Maximus, highly esteemed scholars who search the world over for treasured artifacts, are affiliated at the moment with the La Sapienza in Rome."

"That's a good thing—that everyone does what they're best at or interested in doing—then it doesn't feel like a job. Why do you call yourselves the House of Luceres?"

"Family name. We've been around since the founding of Rome."

My eyes widened. "Wow, amazing. Can you really trace your family tree back that far?"

"We can and we do. I personally have a deep interest in genealogy, shared by a number of us."

"Does Cristaldo find it interesting?" A chance to learn more about Wolfie was not to be missed.

"He does. Very much. He has me look into anyone of Italian heritage we cross paths with."

I felt a wince of discomfort at the possible invasion of my privacy. "My grandparents all come from Italy. Have you looked into me?"

He looked at me with an open expression. The guy seemed so trustworthy. Was it a scam? "Would that bother you if I said I am interested?"

"I don't know. Maybe? But I would prefer to be asked first. Just looking into someone's family without permission is wrong."

"We don't do it to harm anyone. Just to see if we have relatives in remote locations we don't know about."

"Why? So you can share pack wealth with them?" I joked, trying to hide my discomfort. Las Vegas was not turning out at all like I had expected.

"Exactly." He rocked back on his heels, apparently well satisfied with himself.

"What? What do you mean?" My heart literally skipped a beat. I raised a hand to my chest to make sure I was okay.

"I mean precisely that. If you are related to the Luceres, you share in the wealth."

My mind boggled at the implications. "You mean, if it's discovered I have Luceres blood, I get a share of all this?" I waved my hands around myself in disbelief.

"And all the other casinos around the world."

Holy freakin' shit. Had I really heard correctly? I stared at him unblinkingly for a few seconds, trying to sort my thoughts. *Please, dear God, let me be related.* Just thinking what that could mean to my hard-working parents and grandparents threw me into a tizzy. Maybe we could even turn the family business, Mama's Pizza, into a franchise? It was the fondest dream of my parents.

"When will we know for certain?" I finally opened my mouth to ask.

"Soon. I take it I have your permission to pursue all avenues of inquiry?"

"Yes! Of course! And please, keep me posted as to what you find out. I can even call my parents for you. They've kept ties with Italy. They might have the answers you need?"

"It would be more helpful if you keep this to yourself for now. We don't want to get everyone's hopes up if things fall through."

"Good point." That would suck, making my parents think they were coming into immense wealth only to have it taken away from them. Like having the winning lottery ticket jerked out of my hand and sent flying over a cliff into the sea. "My lips are sealed." I dragged an invisible zipper across my lips.

Chapter Twelve

Cristaldo

It seemed to be two steps forward and one back with Everly. We'd been so close earlier today, sharing experiences. I'd enjoyed that very much. And now this, her being difficult again. Why did she not realize I was only trying to keep her safe? Why did she question everything?

At least it gave time for Serge to have the talk with her that he'd promised. Serge had done himself proud, coming up with the idea of sharing the information of how our pack's finances worked, to gain her trust and cooperation. Now, when I shut down the concerts and outings for safety reasons, her friends would go home, but she'd stay. *In my bed.*

After what I'd experienced the night before, seeing her passion and receptive nature as she laid herself open to pleasure and the night sky, I could only imagine what it would be like to have her spread fully just for me, her ass pinked from her punishment for whatever slight infraction occurred, her sex swollen and slick with desire.

"Are you even listening to me?" Lucius asked, his tone annoyed.

"Yes, you were saying that the casino in Cancun has reported a possible sighting of that legendary card counter, the one they call *il camaleonte*?"

"Yes, the Chameleon. Do you want to go there? Take care of it yourself?"

"No. You go. I'm needed here."

"Is it that drummer?" Lucius's eyes narrowed with suspicion though he nodded at my directive.

"What if it is? Someone needs to watch out for her. Until she's proven to be one of us, she's in mortal danger."

"And what if she isn't one of us?"

Only my twin would get away with asking such a traitorous question. Anyone else, I would have taken their head clear off. "She's one of us."

"Fine. I'll leave now and be back soon as I can. I want to be here for the party."

"And I don't want you away during the blood moon. Too dangerous."

"You worried about me, brother? Tell the truth, I'm a lot more worried about you. You haven't been yourself since she showed up. Letting women go without dipping into them. Being a tourist on the Strip. What has the House of Luceres come to? Soon she'll have you so pussy whipped you'll both be inside watching paint dry," he mocked.

I growled in warning. "Don't speak of her again."

"Fine." Lucius walked away, throwing the final words over his back. "Just don't say I didn't warn you."

Five minutes later, I found Everly still chatting with Serge. He nodded at me, giving the signal that all was well, before he left.

"Is everything all right?" she asked.

I wanted to pull her into my arms and make the frown between her eyebrows disappear. "I need to talk with you. Alone."

"Okay, just a sec." She moved away to speak to her bandmates, who glanced over at me with speculation riding high in their eyes. I directed her over to the elevator with every intention of getting her up to the penthouse, where we could have all the privacy we needed. It was time. Time to really get to know *la mia bella ragazza dolce.*

"No. I want my own room on a different floor. You need your space and I need mine."

Where was this coming from? She wouldn't look at me as she said the fighting words.

I shook my head, crossing my arms over my chest. "I won't hear of it. You stay with me."

"Why are you being so difficult? If we're related, it's best we keep apart. I mean, what if we're half-siblings or something weird like that?"

"Then you know I'm looking into your heritage and what that means?"

She nodded. "Doesn't mean you have to look after me. I know women throw themselves at you all the time. I'm not one of them. And I know you own casinos all over the world, for heaven's sake! What are you doing worrying about me?"

"Other women are not you, Everly. Look at me."

She reluctantly stared at me, her expression wary.

"I don't want other women. I want to get to know you."

She glanced away. "I'm only here for a couple more days. Why complicate things? Best I stay in my own room and be with my own kind."

"You *are* my kind. Beautiful, talented and generous to a fault. I'm still the same man that walked out with you today. You enjoyed that, right?"

She looked undecided now, though she nodded once, chewing on a plush bottom lip that I badly wanted to nibble on myself.

"Come. I want to spend time with you. Get to know the real Everly Affini." How did men put up with the small talk necessary to get a confused female into their bed? Though if I managed that tonight, I might have just learned a secret unknown to most men. Never had I had to work so hard to get a female to come to me. It was both intriguing and maddening.

"Fine. But we need to keep our distance. In case we're closely related."

"I can promise you will be a distant relative at best. Nothing that would affect our being together."

"How can you be so sure? What do you know?"

"Get on this elevator and I will tell you all I know about it."

"Fine. But never lie to me. Promise me that. It's a deal-breaker." She gave me a direct look that struck me hard in the gut.

How was I supposed to promise that? I had to lie. To protect her. To protect my pack. *Hell, to protect myself. Damn, what if she finds out about the ruse with Stubbs or all the things I've had to hide from her?* But surely, she'd understand why I *had* to lie? Maybe I could share something. Some part of myself that would get her to know who I really am? What I stand for?

"I promise." I said the simple words with great difficulty, my lips stiffened with resolve. My inner wolf fumed at my weakness. *Remember who you are. Be the alpha — no need to apologize for what has to be. We take what we want. Claim her. Now.*

"I'll hold you to it." She preceded me onto the elevator.

I joined her and stood my ground, my thoughts strengthened by my wolf.

When the doors slid open at Cristaldo's penthouse floor, I hesitated. What the hell was I thinking? This man was so wrong for me. On every level. Social, economic and now maybe related. But how could I fight this man? A man who wanted to give me tons of money if we shared the same heritage. A man I was attracted to like no other.

"Come. Let's have a drink." He offered his hand to me and I stepped off the elevator.

"I need to shower first. I get so hot when I play. I smell right now."

"You smell great." He licked his lips, drawing attention to his mouth. Oh yeah, it was going to be *so* easy to stay away from him.

"I'll be back in a few minutes."

"No need to dress up on my account. Meet me in the lounge, across from the breakfast nook."

"Right." The way he said *talk* was highly suggestive. While a nun's habit might be the most helpful in this situation, it would take a medieval chastity belt to do the job, I wanted him that badly. As soon as we'd been in the elevator, in a confined space where I'd breathed in his tantalizing essence, I had wanted him. His touch, his kiss, his passion.

I barreled down the hallway to my suite, to have a badly needed shower. After our talk, I was excusing myself. *Don't let it go any further than that, Everly.* I kept up my resolve through the shower, through the drying off and even through the choosing of a favorite oriental robe that tied at the waist and flattered with its images of white roses on a deep red background. All my things had shown up in the huge walk-in closet, plus more brand-new clothes and shoes I didn't recognize in my size. I ignored them. All they did was remind me of how far apart Cristaldo and I were in the real world.

I flicked my hair over my shoulders and marched down the hall to join him.

The door to the lounge was closed. I knocked.

"Come in."

I pushed open the door to be greeted by a room right out of Caligula's Rome. Magnificent pale blue silk flowed in silken waterfalls all around the space. Couches that allowed more than one person to lie together. White columns and fancy screens that gave privacy and created alcoves. I could well imagine a Roman orgy happening here. Was that what he thought was going to happen? *Think again, Wolfie.*

He sprawled on one of the sofas, his body now encased in a long royal blue robe, open to the waist and exposing an enviably muscular chest and abs that instantly turned my mouth dry. He held two large glasses of amber liquor that sparkled in the light.

"Come. Drink a toast with me. To us getting to know one another better."

He commanded like a Roman god, his golden aura making my body soften. I moved forward as if in a dream, then took the offering from him and sat down.

I raised the glass to my lips and took an appreciative sip of the fragrant nectar.

"Very nice." I managed the two words, though all my senses screamed at me to get the hell out of there. But I couldn't have walked away from this if my life had depended on it. I was just too drawn to the man.

"Glad you approve." He sounded different now. This was his element, where he was most comfortable. I was right. Our lives were just too far apart.

"Why are we doing this?"

"What do you mean? I thought you wanted to talk?"

"I do. But this is a bit much, don't you think?" I gave a nod to the fantasy land we sat in.

"Why not be comfortable? Money is only meant to be spent to give pleasure. I have enough for a hundred lifetimes. Why not enjoy this one fully?"

"I'm not used to money being spent on anything but the necessities."

"Then all the more reason to enjoy this special time." He waved his hand around, then placed the other one over my shoulders and drew me closer.

I couldn't help myself—I allowed him to pull me up against his hard body. The air in the room seemed to be holding its breath. My pulse climbed even as I knew how bad an idea this was. But something else was at play. Something that I could not fight. It had me in its sway, pulling me out to sea as if in a trance, watching the shoreline vanish from view. I gulped the liquor in an effort to steady myself, but it only heated me more.

"I want to kiss you again. Say you want it too." He ran a finger lightly over the seam of my lips, tantalizing the sensitive flesh. Fighting to breathe, surrounded by his intoxicating scent, his large, virile body causing an acute hunger to grow deep inside me, I felt pushed past control, past endurance, making me reach out to him.

"I want you to kiss me again." The worlds spilled out as if I were in a trance created by a magical spell.

He crushed me to his naked chest. My breasts, bare under the robe, rubbed against his warmth, the peaked nipples pressing into him, begging for attention. My panties flooded with wetness, my sex swollen and needy. I ached for him. So much power filled his hard body, more than I had ever experienced in a man before. But he was no ordinary man. He was a god of war. My being struggled with giving in to him. *Giving in to my wildest desires and fantasies.* My body won in a life-defining moment, for I could not have pulled away if my mortal soul had depended on it.

His lips followed where his finger had been, soft at first, then with an intensity that rocked me. His mouth devoured me. I moaned. I feared him, feared this, but I wanted him more.

He pushed my robe aside with impatient hands and applied his mouth, tightening his lips around a budded nipple. He licked around the sensitive peak, then suddenly drew hard on the vulnerable tip, making me vibrate with need.

"I want to taste you. All of you," he breathed against my breasts. Then he reached under my robe with hands that demanded I submit to his will, and pulled down my panties. When my underwear was free, he raised them to his nose and breathed deeply.

"You smell like heaven." In a flash, he flipped me so that my legs were braced on either side of his body, revealing my mound to his view. I let my legs fall apart farther. I wanted him to see all of me. To see how wet I was for him.

"So perfect, so pretty." He gazed hungrily at my nakedness before he dipped a finger between the folds as if giving thanks. He found my clit and began to massage it in tantalizing circular motions.

I moaned, unable to deny how turned on I was. When he applied his mouth to my core, the nerve endings tingled and sprang to life, vibrating as I was thrust into a world of pure sensation. A world which was all about gratification and desire. I couldn't think. My clit was swollen and aching and my thighs slickened with the fluid that spilled from me.

He lapped it up, sweeping his raspy tongue along my inner lips, dipping into my channel and licking deep within me. Using his talented hands against clenched tissue, he stroked, working his fingers inside me as violent pleasure lashed me. All the while he sucked and nipped at my clit. It was too much. I went to push him away, but he continued, overriding my weak objections.

"Feel it all, baby. Ride my hand. Take what you need."

His voice threw me over the edge. I opened to him, let him feel all my pent-up desire. *Just. For. Him.* And when I could not take any more of his expert fingers stretching and rubbing against and in me, the throbbing increased to a crescendo and I spiraled into the abyss, falling completely apart.

I opened my eyes in wonder some time later. I blushed when I realized how wanton I had been. How I had let myself be so exposed to him.

He smiled down at me as I still lay sprawled before him, unashamed in all my glory, a wide, wolfish smile that make my heart lose a full beat. I glanced down at the apex of his strong golden thighs, where his cock jutted through the robe, begging to be kissed.

I smiled back. "My turn."

Chapter Thirteen

Cristaldo

Everly threw off her robe and got to her knees on the floor in front of me in one amazing, graceful movement. She licked her lips and crawled toward me, her naked breasts perfect globes that swayed back and forth with each tiny movement.

I leaned forward, bound her long silky locks in one hand and tugged her pretty mouth toward me.

"You want it?" I asked, grabbing my cock with my other hand and guiding it toward her sweet lips. She nodded, staring at my swollen member. I thrust into her mouth, her lips parting as the broad crest pressed against them, her tongue catching the essence of the mating hormone seeping from the glands beneath. Her mouth closed over me, silk on steel.

A helpless moan escaped her throat as she sucked eagerly at my engorged hardness. She drew on it, her cheeks moving with the effort, giving herself up to the lust flaming through her body.

"That's it. Suck me. Take it all." She tightened her mouth at the explicit language, reaching one hand down to cup my balls.

My cock filled her mouth and I pushed toward the back of her throat. Her hands busy with my balls, I reached for a nipple, which jutted out so wonderfully from her swollen breasts. I took over the rhythm, thrusting in long strokes past her lips, knowing my expression was savage with lust.

She moaned. I twisted her nipple and she moaned harder.

"I should punish you for making me wait so long." I let go of her hair and smacked her ass, still playing with her nipple.

She arched her back, giving better access, and I hit the other rounded globe with more force. I reached between her legs and found her soaking wet, her lips extended and wide open, her clit swollen and defiant. I thrust three fingers into her, stretching her. She'd need to be stretched as far as possible to take my extreme girth.

"You like that. When I punish you." It was not a question but a truth. Her arousal had sharpened, nearly killing me with the instant need to possess her.

She couldn't hold back her moans as she milked the sensitive head of my member with her mouth. I tightened my fingers in her hair again, directing her. I gave her another heady taste of the hormone-rich cum. Her body sensitized further, her mouth becoming greedier.

"Ah, baby, that's it. Take all of me. Your mouth is amazing." I chose words to goad her on, and, made hungry for me, she sucked all the harder, drawing me deeper into her throat. But I wanted more. I wanted to sink into that sweet pink pussy of hers. I could not allow myself to brand her mine, not yet, but I could make her want only me, the only one who would be able to satisfy her. I longed to stretch her until it was only me who could give her what she needed.

When I was about to come, I pulled out of her mouth. "I want you now. Open for me."

I grabbed her hips and held her upward, straddling me. I teased her soaking wet lips and clit with the thick head of my cock, sliding back and forth down her swollen slit. Her breathing became ragged, her skin hotter and more flushed. She was so ready that she was losing control.

She reached down and held herself open, pulling her lips wide apart, exposing her pink pussy. Heat pulsed as my precum slicked her entrance, the elixir guaranteeing her nerve endings would burn with a desperate need to be touched, to be rubbed against. Submissive, she had no control, had given it all over to me, her alpha.

When she whimpered, I pushed as far as I could into her in one long satisfying stroke, and even then it was not all of me. Her warmth surrounded me, hot and squeezing.

"So tight," I murmured, losing myself for a moment in the sensation. I was so thick, so huge, that I gave her a moment to recover, then began to thrust myself in time with her movements. She was a dream come true.

"Harder," she said.

I needed no other invitation. I buried myself right to the hilt inside her, breaking through whatever restriction remained.

She screamed and scratched my back, digging her nails in as my cock tore through her.

"Are you okay?"

"Perfect," she said, her voice low and throaty. I reached up and tugged on her nipples, making her squeal and push herself harder against me. Wetness flooded out of her and I wanted to lap it up. She smelled, felt and tasted of heaven. I rubbed myself harder against her clit, savoring the cream it brought.

I dimly remembered that I had to keep myself in check or I would bite her, mark her mine, so every other male could smell my scent on her. I couldn't do that yet. Not to her, though every cell in my body screamed to finish it, desperate to experience the knotting with her, to swell fully inside her and bind her to me. My very own Forever Mate.

Chapter Fourteen

Everly

My mental fog lifted and I pulled my robe together with shaking hands. What had I just let happen? The very thing I'd promised myself I would stay away from — throwing myself at a man who would only hurt me, who would move on when our time here was over.

My body throbbed with the memory of what we had just done, my ass still warm from his hand, my breasts aching from all the attention. And walking? That was out of the question.

"I'm going to wash you," he said, picking me up, a naked warrior carrying his prize.

"No, I'm fine," I protested, trying to squirm out of his arms.

"You'll need the warmth of water to ease the ache. You were a wild woman, *tesoro*."

I turned my face in to his chest so he couldn't see how red I had to be. My whole body felt hot with the realization of how much I had already submitted to this man. What was going on with me? And after I'd promised myself not to do this.

He carried me across the room and tugged open a drape to a Roman-like spa area behind sliding glass doors. He slid one panel open to reveal a large sunken pool with crystal-clear water showing off its tiled blue-and-white mosaic pattern, wisps of steam rising lazily off the surface. Chaise lounges were strategically placed between lovely white marble statues of water nymphs at play around the perimeter. Stacks of fluffy white towels filled the shelves.

"Set me down. I can walk." *Maybe.*

"I will wash you." His tone defied any more objections.

"Fine. Go for it."

He set me down at the side of the pool of water on a soft, thick mat, tugged off my robe, then placed me into the warm water as though I were a small child. I lay back, letting the warmth soothe my tender flesh, my hair floating around me like long strands of seaweed. The water level, shallow at this end, barely covered my breasts.

He got in beside me, the water displaced by his huge body rising and flowing over my chest.

We lay side by side. I kicked at the water a bit with my heels, enjoying the small splashes. I closed my eyes, the enticing warmth seeping into my consciousness and relaxing me like nothing had ever done after a concert. Or maybe it was the soul-shattering sex? *Whatever.* I was going to insist on bathing more instead of showering from now on.

As much as I wanted to fall asleep, to forget this wild night, I was far too aware of the man so silent at my side. Even with my eyes closed, I sensed him there, my body far too aware of what he could do to me. *Turn me inside out with lust.* I swallowed. This was beginning to feel too much like a fever dream. All this...it just couldn't be real. I desperately needed something tangible to ground myself.

"Tell me about yourself, Cristaldo. Something I don't know."

He cleared his throat. "What do you want to know? We just made love — isn't that enough to show you who I am, what we can be together?"

"Sex is not the only thing that matters. I might not be here for long, but I'd like to get to know you a bit better. Maybe after we leave when the concert is over tomorrow, we can stay in touch? And if I know more about you, it gives us something to talk about. Or maybe you don't do that? Stay in touch with women you take to your bed?" I detested the idea of another female sharing his bed, but a man like Cristaldo? He obviously had his pick.

"You're not leaving me."

Stunned, I sat up straighter. "What are you talking about? Of course I'm leaving. I can't abandon my band, my family...I have to go home."

He reached out and grasped my breasts, exposed now that I had moved higher in the water. Expertly massaging them, he pinched the nipples, sending an ache of pleasure into my pussy so powerful that I gasped. I throbbed with the instant need to be filled yet again. I tried not to show how much he was affecting me, but I failed. *Miserably.*

"These are mine. All mine." He moved his hand lower, cupping my mound, then thrust his fingers inside me, stretching me. "This is mine. Only mine."

"Taking it all a bit far, aren't we?" I said, trying to lighten my response but only hearing the nervousness in my voice. Uncertain if this was his usual after-sex talk, I was almost afraid to look at him.

"No. Not far enough."

What in the hell does that even mean? "I-I've had one jealous lover. I don't need another."

"I never let go of what is mine." His voice held a dangerous edge that I had never heard him use before. For the first time, fear sliced through me.

I scrambled away from him then, the water flying as I pulled myself to my feet by the side of the pool, my body's discomfort forgotten.

"I have to go." Though the words were unnecessary — they spilled out. I ran, not caring of how I appeared to him, naked and desperate.

"Everly, come back! You misunderstand the situation."

Oh, I think I get it! I stomped all the way back to my suite, then began to pack, ignoring my bare-naked and soaking-wet state.

The door burst open and a naked Cristaldo confronted me. When he saw what I was doing, his expression turned to one of confusion. "You're leaving me? After what we just shared?"

"You went too far, saying you won't let me leave. I don't do that. I *won't* do that. Never again." I packed as I half-shouted at him, throwing the few clothes that would fit into the carryall. The rest could stay.

His expression darkened. "I keep you here for your own good. To keep you safe."

"You keep saying that, but I'm not asking that of you." I whirled on him. "I need to make my own way in this world. Not that I don't appreciate your wanting me to be safe, but I've been managing that all by myself up until now."

"Things have changed. You don't understand the threat."

"Then tell me."

His expression told the tale for him.

"I thought so. You won't open up and share anything that would help me understand what the hell's going on here."

He sat and patted the bed with one hand, his actions asking me to join him. I hesitated, uncertain.

"I'll tell you what I can, without causing any security issues for my extended family. All right?"

"Okay. Spill." I sat down on a chair across the room, my spine stiffened by my resolve.

"I had a younger sister. Mia. She was so full of life. So beautiful." His eyes bored into mine with a bleakness that touched my soul. *'Had a sister.'* Oh. My. God. A piece of the puzzle dropped into place. The anguish I'd glimpsed when he'd fixed my hair came back to me.

I got up and joined him on the bed, taking his hand.

"She fell in love with the wrong guy. A member of another house. But they were so young, thinking they were invincible, certain that in modern times, the old ways don't apply. They were attacked one night when they'd both snuck out to be together, by a Nomad—a stranger to both our houses. They were murdered— torn to shreds." He stopped talking and took his head into his hands, his voice raw with grief. "I can never forgive myself for not knowing what she was up to. For not protecting her."

It was far worse than I had imagined. My heart squeezed hard in sympathy. "But how could you know? Nobody could know."

"Don't you see? It's my job to know. To protect my family."

I put my arm around him, feeling the pain and sorrow escaping from his body.

"I understand now your need to protect others. But you don't have to worry so much about me. I don't take chances." Then I realized how foolish that sounded. I was taking a chance right now. Naked and alone with a man I had the hots for…and feeling something more for him that only spelled trouble.

"Will you stay? With me?"

I swallowed, hearing the cost of his asking in his tone. A man like Cristaldo did not beg, had no need to. I didn't understand it—*I mean, why me?* But I respected him more at that moment than ever before. To share something that had wounded him so badly meant a great deal. For some reason, he trusted me.

"Yes, I'll stay, for now."

"Thank you."

He pulled me into his arms and hugged me tight. Through his chest, the strong beat of his heart aligned with mine, a sensation of being in sync me that filled me with a strange emotion. Uncomfortable, I held on to myself with great difficulty.

"I need to sleep," I said.

"Of course." He surprised me by letting me go with a chaste kiss on the forehead and a playful slap on my ass. When he'd gone, I slowly unpacked, thinking of all I'd learned. *Money. Essential, but it doesn't protect a person from tragedy.*

After drying my hair, I slipped into bed, hoping to sleep. But my dreams were haunted by images of wolves prowling a barren landscape. I tossed and turned, caught in the throes of worry and sympathy for the past that could not be changed. *Nomad.* The word he'd used to describe his sister's murderer rose in my mind. A lone killer attacking two young lovers turned the marrow in my bones to ice. *How could such a thing happen?*

I awoke blurry-eyed and unprepared for the day, my body still tender from our lovemaking.

My phone rang and I wearily reached over to pick it up to check the ID of the caller. I sat up straighter. *Constable Perkins? What's he doing calling me in Vegas?* We'd had some interactions over Jason when he'd suggested the restraining order. Maybe it was something to do with what was going on now? The thought energized me and I quickly answered the call. He'd always promised to call if he had information for me.

"Morning, Constable," I said.

"Miss Affini. I hope I didn't wake you?" His familiar accent filled me with thoughts of Surrey and being home. Watching my mother serve pizza to happy customers. *I can't possibly be homesick yet, can I?*

"No, I was awake, but I'm curious as to why you're calling?"

"It's about Jason Stubbs."

My heart rate jacked up. "What about him? Has he been picked up for being in Vegas? For threatening me?"

"Vegas? Can't be. We arrested him in Vancouver two days ago on drug and gun charges and a serious assault of an officer. He's going away for a long time. I just wanted to call to reassure you that you have nothing to worry about from him. The judge will not be granting bail in his case."

"What? I had no idea. I thought he'd followed me to Vegas and was threatening me here?" Cristaldo had lied to me. I wasn't in any danger at all. The knowledge hit me like a sledgehammer. The *one* thing I'd asked him never to do was lie to me. *Lying is a deal breaker. Crap. My judgment in men sucks.*

"Not sure where you got that idea. But I'm telling you, he's in custody. No longer a threat to you or anyone else."

"I appreciate you taking the time to tell me. I do feel much safer knowing."

"You're welcome. By the way, congratulations on winning the contest. You're doing Surrey proud."

"Thank you, and thanks for calling." My voice sounded far away as my head filled with a loud buzzing sensation and my vision narrowed.

"Good day. Be well, Miss Affini."

I ended the call with nerveless fingers. My throat dry, I jumped out of bed. The sooner I was out of this penthouse and away from its owner, the better.

Chapter Fifteen

Cristaldo

A knock sounded on the door of my office and I looked up from the endless paperwork I insisted on handling myself, though I had more accountants than I could count. The pun made me snort. *An alpha must always keep his hand on the throttle.*

"Come in. What is it?" I barked.

"I have some good news, sire." Serge popped his head in, a nervous smile flitting across his features.

"Tell me the good news." By his tone, I knew it wasn't all good news.

"It's about Miss Affini."

My heart rate jacked up. I set aside the report I was working on and gave him my full attention. "What about her?"

"Her lab test results are in and she's one of us."

"And?"

He hesitated for a second. "She's got a very rare genetic sequence. One that we haven't seen in decades."

"For Christ's sake, man, cut to the chase."

"She's a dual breed. She can be mated to either house."

"*Damn*! Does the House of Ribelle know?" This complicated things even as it made her rarer than the finest treasure the world has to offer.

"No, it's all been done in complete secrecy. They will have had to run their own tests to know. What are you going to do? The rules say—"

"To hell with the rules. I'm claiming her."

Serge looked stricken, his face gone pale. "Sire, you know that could lead to problems. A war with the House of Ribelle is the last thing we need right now. The blood moon's already causing outbreaks of hostility between the houses. You saw how the stage was breached last night at the end of the concert?"

"There won't be another concert. I'm canceling. Find another band to replace them."

"Whatever you think best. But to avoid a bloodbath, I beg you not to rush this thing. You can mate her, claim her yours, *after* you win the challenge. What's a couple of days? Then she will be yours forever."

"No! Absolutely not! She's mine."

I would go to her. I had the green light now. My biting and marking her would not harm her in any way. She would *never* have to go through a painful transition that so many humans without the special gene had to endure and so often did not survive, though Alessandro and Maximus had recently announced that they had a lead on the priceless artifact to assist a human during the change—the famed Lupus Sanguis chalice, made from the original wolf's blood and bone and spoken of in legends.

I had private doubts that such a thing really existed or, if it did, would work after being buried in a secret location for millennia. But if it contained enough DNA after all these years and effected a transformation, its price was beyond compare.

Of course, I would be the one to take the brunt of my actions once the House of Ribelle found out I'd circumvented the rules. But hell, who cared? She was meant to be mine. Fate had sent her here to be my chosen one.

* * * *

What was that? I stilled, my breathing hitched, listening with all my being, putting one hand protectively to the belt of knives I wore around my waist. When no sound followed, I began to tiptoe down the hallway again. The sooner I was away from this place, the better. I prayed I wouldn't run into Sly or any of the staff who kept the penthouse running so smoothly. I just knew they'd hurry straight to him with the tale.

When the doors closed, my breath whooshed from my body. I slumped against the wall of the elevator, grateful that I'd gotten away unseen. The last thing I wanted was a confrontation. I'd told him how things stood with me. That lying was a game changer. But even so, doubts crept in when I thought of how much he had been through with his sister. I shook my head. *No.* It still didn't make it right. Besides, we had no future. He came from a world I barely understood, all glamor like having a majordomo, for heaven's sake.

And most likely taking what he wanted before discarding it for the challenge of something new. I'd soon be forgotten and a new woman would take my place in his bed. The idea pained me more than it should, but I had to suck it up. That was the way the real world worked.

When the bell dinged, announcing the lobby, I made myself straighten up and pulled my hoodie around my face. I was getting away from this place none too soon, before it was too late and I fell harder for Cristaldo. The compulsion to leave had grabbed such complete control of me that my body felt rigid, my muscles tense.

I had to zigzag my way across the packed lobby floor, my carryall tucked under one arm. The outside world called to me as I was swept with the current onto the sidewalk with a crowd of people who seemed to be part of a tour group. Happy and animated, they were obviously looking forward to their day. I desperately wanted to go with them, sit on a bus and let a guide tell me about all the attractions in Vegas. Such simple fun, now that I didn't need to worry about Jason Stubbs anymore. Damn, how could Cristaldo have lied about that? Scaring me into thinking the guy was after me, just so he could take advantage? *No.* Stop thinking about *him.*

The powerful urge to get completely away overcame me and I turned to an older couple standing near me. "Is this a private tour or can anyone pay to go along?"

"It's not private, dear. We're just going to see a few more of the casinos around town. It should be fun and it doesn't cost much. The driver has the tickets," the older man said, his wife nodding and beaming at his side.

Excellent.

I approached the uniformed driver who stood near the side of the bus, checking that people were meant to be on the tour.

"Could I buy a ticket?"

"Sure, I got a couple left." He reached in his pocket and drew out a card. "Thirty dollars get you into five top casinos and a beverage."

"That sounds good. Thanks." I pulled the cash from my bag and we exchanged items.

I climbed the steps and entered the front of the bus, finding a seat beside an elderly woman. We shared a quick smile of greeting. This was better. Taking charge of my own day without interference. I pulled out my cell phone while I waited for the bus to get moving, texted Cleo and Layla to let them know I'd be back in a few hours, that I just needed some alone time. Not that uncommon for me on tour. I added that Jason Stubbs had been in jail for a couple of days and was no longer a threat to any of us. I didn't want them to worry.

I immediately got a ping. A text from Cleo.

Did Cristaldo lie to you about Jason?

Yes, but it does mean that there's nothing to worry about, I texted back.

Still sucks. See you later.

Xxoo

Satisfied that things were moving in a positive direction, I slipped my cell phone into my bag and leaned back, closing my eyes.

"Do you like to gamble, hon?"

I opened my eyes to discover the white-haired senior was eyeing me with interest.

"Never really did it much. Just a few lottery tickets. You?"

"Oh no. I never gamble, well, unless it's free, then all bets are off," she said with a coy smile. "I just go for something to do. It's a fine tour and I've met so many nice people."

"How often do you go?"

"About once a month. I bring my knitting along and sit and people watch. I love to imagine what they do for a living by their choice of clothing. Footwear alone speaks volumes."

"That's an interesting hobby." She reminded me of my grandmother, still filled with enthusiasm about meeting new people.

The bus pulled away from the curb and into traffic.

"We're going to do a little change-up for today's tour, folks. First up, Casino Ribelle, the towering complex visible at the far end of the Strip. For this special event, they're providing a twenty-dollar chip to each person on tour as their thanks for visiting and passing on the good word."

"Oh, isn't that nice of them!" My seatmate's eyes sparkled with glee. "I guess it's because we've never visited them before. At least in my memory."

"You can have my chip as well."

"Well, land's sakes, thank you. Aren't you a darling?"

A movement to my right drew my attention. A guy had picked up his phone and was texting so quickly that his fingers were nearly a blur. He looked up at me as I watched, his eyes filled with speculation. A shiver snaked down my spine for some unknown reason.

"Cold, dear?"

"No. I'm fine." But I couldn't help look over at the man every few seconds...and each time he was staring right back at me. I grew more uncomfortable by the minute. As soon as we got to the Ribelle Casino, I was making sure to keep away from the likes of him.

Five minutes later, our destination reached, I joined the others in disembarking the bus. I hurried inside, keeping my distance from the creepy guy.

"Miss, oh, miss, your free chip."

I took it from a man who had a nametag pinned to his shirt and a wide smile pasted on his face, then looked around for my seatmate to pass it on to her. *Ah.* There she was, near the fountain. The area had lots of seating and other seniors were sitting there as well. I took a look around as I walked over. It was a spectacular casino, rivalling the Glitter Palace.

"Thank you, dear." She beamed at me. "I'll play in a bit. Care to join me in some people watching?"

"No, thanks. I think I'd like to walk around."

I took the first walkway to the right, skirting the huge bank of gambling machines that were being pressed into service by the gray-haired set. What else did the casino have to offer? A coffee bar would not be amiss. In my headlong rush to get away from the penthouse, I hadn't had the essential nectar of the gods. My stomach rumbled, reminding me that wasn't all I had missed.

Rounding yet another corner of the labyrinth in my search for a kiosk or lounge and to keep away from the asshole who still dogged me, I realized I wasn't headed the right way. *And I thought that food and drink would be easy to come by in Vegas, right next to gambling.* Retracing my steps, I was acutely aware that there was no one else in sight at the moment, not even the annoying creepy guy who had gotten me lost in the first place.

A floor plan would not go amiss. I took out my phone and was busy scrolling down the app list when I was suddenly aware of someone in my personal space.

"Miss Affini. Welcome to the House of Ribelle."

A group of half a dozen men confronted me, a line-up of linebackers that immediately had my full and undivided attention.

"How do you know my name?" I looked each man in the face in turn, letting them know they weren't intimidating me, even though they totally were.

"Are you not the drummer in The Sirens, playing in Nero's?"

"Yes. Who are you?"

"I'm Thaddeus and this is Rocco." All the men were attired in dark clothing and looked like they were used to having their orders go unquestioned. The one called Thaddeus had a dark mane of hair just beginning to thread with gray, while Rocco had a close-cropped cut, along with tattoos visible on his thick neck and peeking out of the cuff of his suit jacket. His defiant look while staring directly at me was the most alarming of the group.

"I was just trying to find a coffee bar and seems I got lost in this place. You should market an app so people can find their way around in here."

"Of course. We'll look into it. It would be an honor to offer you refreshments, Miss Affini, and to listen to more of your ideas for improvement."

"Ah, no, but thank you. Just point out a spot and I'll get right out of your hair." I adopted a breezy tone, wishing fervently that another human being would chance by.

"Nonsense. What kind of a host would I be if I let the amazing drummer from The Sirens not be taken proper care of? And in my own casino. No, I insist." He shook his large head, his dark eyes glittering with an intensity I wasn't entirely comfortable with.

I didn't really have a choice. I could run, but that might be a bit extreme in the circumstances. Surely the owners of a casino had to be careful? And others knew I was here. "Fine. But I'll need to dine and dash. I'm fairly certain my tour bus is going to load soon."

"We'll have you back in lots of time to connect with your tour. Have no fear." His words reassured me.

I stepped forward to join the men, and in seconds I was surrounded, as if they were my own personal bodyguards.

"Aw, guys, could you step back a bit? Give a person room to breathe?"

The group was moving more quickly now and I was bumped from behind by one of the men, hedging me in even tighter.

"Excuse me. What's the rush?"

There was dead silence. In a matter of seconds, I was hustled into a side room. The door shut with a loud bang and I swore I heard the lock click.

Chapter Sixteen

Cristaldo

"How the hell did she just walk right out of the casino and no one stopped her? Something or someone had to have been mind-working on her. Those damn Ribelle curs are behind this, I'm certain of it." I glared at Serge.

He stood solemn and respectful in front of my desk, the bearer of bad news. The House of Ribelle was known for fucking around in a potential mate's mind, luring her to them. It was one of their strengths, making them a formidable pack and enemy. I ignored the slight hit of guilt for knowing I had pulled the same stunt on Everly a day earlier. It was different and excusable. *I'm her Forever Mate.*

He sighed. "Apparently she slipped out when a tour group was preparing to board a bus to visit some of the casinos."

"Where is she now?" I got up and paced the floor. I had to do something to get her safely under my roof again. The thought sent my brain into a frenzy of worry and pain. Rocco might mark her first and she would be lost to me. *Forever.*

"We don't know. But we're looking into it. I'm certain we'll be able to track her down without causing an incident."

"Who cares about an incident? This is my Forever Mate we're talking about! I'll burn this town to cinders before I'll let anyone touch a hair on her head."

"With all due respect, I'd advise against it, sire. We need the cooperation of both houses to keep the peace. She's going to turn up soon. I'm positive of it. You know women—she probably just needed some time alone. Did you have an argument or anything like that? Maybe she left for her own reasons and not because the Ribelle called her?"

"No. Nothing. She came willingly to my bed last night. I was ready to claim her my mate her after you called, but she was gone."

"What did her friends say?"

"Just that she wanted to go for a walk. Do you think they know more?" I narrowed my eyes in thought. "Maybe we should question them again?"

"I'll take care of it. We don't want to scare them off."

Serge cleared his throat, the signal that he had more to say.

"Yes?"

"Even if they've taken her, and that's a big if, they won't harm her. But they will challenge you."

"A challenge I can handle. But what if—" I couldn't say it out loud.

"No. No fear of that. A violation of that magnitude is a serious offense. It is forbidden under pack law." The words hung between us, a warning of how costly such an infraction would be to their house. Or ours. "Restitution of the highest order would be called for, and their pack is not in a financial position to pay. They've been through a great deal of expansion these past few years trying to keep up with your success and it's been costly. So it will come down to a challenge. Most likely held during Lupercalia. Much as I would advise against it." Serge gave a grimace of distaste. "But traditions die hard for our kind."

"Too hard."

"I'll go and see her friends now. It's good that you realize the error of storming the casino if she has wandered that far afield. She could be hurt if you charged in without thought of her safety."

"Careful. She's my chosen. I would never harm her." But he had a valid point. I had to temper my wolf. We no longer lived in the time of the dire wolves or berserkers. Challenge had replaced the formidable actions of old, when storming an enemy's position was vital. But the veneer of civilization was thin. If I wasn't careful, I might shed social conventions in a heartbeat. *If my wolf has his way.*

* * * *

"What's the meaning of this?" I demanded, though fear crept through my anger.

"Have a seat," Thaddeus said, gesturing with a polite wave of his hand.

There was only one seat not taken, right in front of him. The room was empty — even the bodyguards had left us alone. *What the hell is going on?*

"You must be wondering why you're here?"

I gave him my best frigid stare. "If you think this is the proper etiquette to getting to know someone, you're sadly mistaken."

"I heard you had spunk. Good. You'll need it."

"What is that supposed to mean?"

"Sit down. I have a lot to tell you. It's time you knew. Now that it's been confirmed."

"I'll stand, thanks." I crossed my arms over my chest.

"Suit yourself. But it's going to take a while. Would you care for a drink?" He sat behind an imposing bit of furniture, his hands tented on the desktop, his lips pursed. This guy wore power like a second skin.

"I thought that was why we were here in the first place?" I shook my head.

"Coffee or something stronger?"

"Coffee. Black." I sat, because standing while he was seated made me feel like I was about to be reprimanded by the school principal.

While I was still studying the layout of the room, noting no windows or any doors leading off the approximately twenty-by-thirty-foot space, the door clicked open and in walked a uniformed waiter carrying an engraved silver carafe of coffee and two porcelain cups on a tray. I looked toward the door he'd come in, wondering if I should make a break for it when he left.

The waiter set the items down, blocking my view of the door, then poured two cups, and placed one in front of me. I could just throw it in his face and make a run for it?

"I have no wish to harm you, Miss Affini, if that's what you're concerned about. I just think there are important things you should be aware of…things that have a bearing on your new life in Vegas."

"What new life in Vegas? I'm just here for a few concerts." My breath hitched in my chest. What the hell was he talking about? While I sat stupefied, the waiter departed and I lost my chance.

"Things don't always work out the way we planned. You will be staying on for the foreseeable future. Has Cristaldo Luceres not shared that with you yet?"

My mind went back over the past couple of days. He had been saying I was his, that he would never let me go, but… I licked my lips, my mind in turmoil. I suddenly wished I had stayed where I was and not ventured out today. I hated that the man across from me, sitting so self-possessed, was making me question things. I tried a sip of coffee, trying to ground myself with the familiar, soothing fragrance and taste. "You can't make such a pronouncement and not tell me what's going on," I demanded.

"Are you aware of the myth of the founding of Rome? The twins, Romulus and Remus, raised by wolves?"

"Vaguely. What does an ancient myth have to do with my not going home? That makes absolutely no sense." I set my cup down with a bang and some of the hot liquid splashed out onto the desk's mirrored surface, narrowly missing burning my hand. I busied myself with sopping it up with a thick linen napkin engraved with the initials of the casino.

"Do you believe there are more mysterious events and creatures on Earth than meets the eye?" He gave me a piercing look, his eyes hooded and dark.

"It's a big world. So yes, strange things have happened over its history. By creatures, you mean like Bigfoot up in Canada? That kind of thing?"

"Hmm, maybe. I was thinking more along the line of werewolves."

"Werewolves!" I began to laugh. I was probably hysterical, or maybe having some kind of out-of-body experience. "No, I don't believe in them."

"You should. We exist."

Was this man sitting so confidently before me, drinking coffee and telling me a fairy tale, insane? I shook my head. He couldn't believe such things. *Could he?*

Floored, I wasn't certain how to respond.

"I know it's a lot to take in, but that doesn't make it any less true." He poured himself another cup of coffee with aplomb, as though the hardest part of the conversation was over. *Yeah, right!* He gestured with the pot at me. I nodded.

"Now, we come to the proof," he said.

"Proof. You think proof exists of…of werewolves?" I found it difficult to even say the word.

"I know it exists. It's written in our DNA code. Yours too."

I choked and spat out a mouthful of coffee. "You think I'm a werewolf! That's crazy!"

"I assure you we have proof. Lab tests. You have the markers of an ancient race written in your genetics. I received your results earlier this morning. It's amazing what a little blackmail and surveillance can achieve. Did you know electronic devices come so small these days you can fit one in a capped tooth?" He chuckled, then reached into his pocket and pulled out a folded piece of paper. "Would you care to see what my foresight bought me?"

"Yes." I strangled out the one-word answer, my mind racing in turmoil. Was this guy crazy enough to want to harm me? I had to get away as soon as the opportunity presented itself and he needed to be locked up for his own good. *No person in their right mind says they're a werewolf and then suggests I'm one as well.*

Was this the danger that Cristaldo had meant? Not Jason Stubbs, but the owners of the Ribelle Casino? Then why the hell not warn me? Why let me think Jason was the threat? And what did this nutcase want with me? It made no sense. My head was swimming with the frightening thoughts going round and round like the world's scariest carousel.

I leaned forward and made myself take the piece of white paper from his outstretched fingers, like I was taking any of this seriously.

Smoothing out the creases, I tried to read it, but none of it made sense. It wasn't as if it was stamped with the word *werewolf.*

"I don't get this. What am I looking for?"

"Yes, it's all a bit much for the layman. Take a look at the bottom. It says dual breed and means you have an extra chromosome."

I did as he suggested. "Okay. That's a weird term. Dual breed. What does that even mean?" I couldn't believe I was discussing such things in such a proper manner, but if he believed it, he could turn on a person in a second. I needed to be careful. *Stay alert.*

"Means you can be mated to either house, House of Luceres or House of Ribelle, without harm. We will challenge for you. At the Lupercalia."

My head was spinning and I swayed a bit in my chair. *Can coffee make a person drunk?* "What exactly is the Lupercalia?"

"Ah, an ancient festival where challenges for mating are often settled. It will have to be changed to neutral territory this year, of course."

"Of course." Did he have any idea how insane his story was? I bit my inner lip, drawing blood that flooded my tongue, proving I wasn't dreaming the whole thing. I had fallen down a rabbit hole so deep that I was itching to make a run for it down any given side tunnel. But I needed to keep my cool. Surely a guy this out of it would make a mistake?

"Well, as interesting as this has all been, I must be going." I set the paper down on his desk, stood and held out my hand. "Very nice to meet you, Mr. Thaddeus."

He pursed his lips. "You're not going anywhere. I don't trust Cristaldo not to mark you before the challenge...even further than he already has. Please, sit down."

I remained standing. As much as I wanted to know what he meant, I couldn't take in any more intel. My mind already rejected what it had heard.

"You are aware that this is illegal? Keeping me here?"

"If you were human, yes, it would be illegal." How can such a madman sound so logical? His calmness was screwing with my brain.

"Are you saying werewolves have no rights?"

He looked nonplused. "You are an interesting shifter. You are going to be a worthwhile asset to my pack, and not just for breeding purposes."

"*What* did you just say?" I'd had enough. More than enough. *Breeding purposes* went past endurance, even for the patience I would normally show someone who had a mental problem. "I'm leaving. Now!"

I pulled a knife out of the band from around my waist and held it out, steady and sure and pointed right at his heart. I could throw it and end this right now. But I didn't want to. I just wanted him to stand down and let me out of this insanity.

"Is that silver?" He didn't even blink.

"Why does everyone keep asking that? No, it's not. But it cuts better than silver."

"I doubt that. Only silver can harm us. Or cutting off our heads. And I don't think you have it in you to cut off my head. Do you, Miss Affini?" His eyes glittered with interest.

"I don't want to hurt you. But I will. Let me out of here!"

"Looks like you're going to need more proof, Miss Affini."

I stared him down. "If you don't open the door right now, you will give me no choice." I gestured with my knife. "Now move. I have deadly aim, and I will launch this at you."

He laughed. *Oh God*, he was even crazier than I thought. What was I supposed to do now? He was pushing me into a tight corner.

"This is your last warning. I swear. I will throw it. It will harm you." I moved into a solid stance, prepared to do what must be done.

"Go ahead. Throw it. See what happens. It may be the proof you need." The flesh around his eyes and mouth tightened, his eyes unblinking.

Damn it. Why was he goading me? Did he want to have to go to the hospital?

"I swear it. Open the door!"

"No. That is not going to happen. You're staying with us until this thing is decided."

"Then you give me no choice."

"Apparently not. Do you have the courage? To throw it?"

His words taunted me. With hot fear cramping my belly, I launched the first knife at his shoulder. I wanted only to wound him, to give me time to escape.

The knife zinged right by him and stuck in the wall. Had he moved? My aim had been true. I slid out another knife and pointed it at him.

"Open the door!"

"No."

I threw the second knife, closer to his mid-section. There was a slight stirring of the air and that knife too missed, sticking in the wall behind him. What the hell was going on? They should both have hit him.

I drew out a third knife.

"I can do this all day, Miss Affini. My reflexes are honed from years of experience. You will not hit me, and if you do—"

I launched the knife before he could possibly be prepared. This time it hit him, dead center of his chest. *Oh, God no!* That had likely been a heart shot and now he was going to die on me.

Unable to stop myself, I rushed forward to help him.

"Why did you make me do that to you?" I asked, bending down in front of him to see what I could do.

The knife stuck out a couple of inches from his jacket. He had to be in tremendous pain.

"You mean this?" He pulled the knife out of his chest as if it was nothing, just a little blood welling up. "It's not silver. You said so yourself. It can't harm our kind."

What the hell? "How is that even possible?" I heard the shock in my voice.

"I'm a werewolf. We're all like this. You too — once you shift for the first time. Healing quickly is one of the best by-products of our genetic anomaly. Of course, it makes one hungrier. Care for some lunch?"

I stepped away from Thaddeus. Now what? Okay, there had to be a magic part to this. I was in Vegas, the apex of sleight of hand and trickery. Just because he was likely wearing some kind of bulletproof vest didn't prove anything. But why was he doing this? To me?

I sat back down on my side of the desk to gather myself.

"What would you like?"

"What do you mean?"

"For lunch. I'm having a thick beefsteak with all the trimmings. I'd recommend it. Followed a nice slab of hot apple pie with two scoops of French vanilla ice cream. One of the best parts of being a werewolf is that consuming more calories is essential."

"Are you insane?" The question popped out before I could hold it back. Maybe it was time to go for broke. "You must be wearing some kind of device so I couldn't push the knife in far enough. Prove to me you're not." Of course, he couldn't, but maybe it would put an end to this charade.

"Certainly." He opened his jacket, removed his tie and unbuttoned his shirt to expose a thick muscular chest with a great deal of body hair. Heck, maybe he was a werewolf, if being hirsute was one of the signs? But Cristaldo…his chest had just the perfect amount of hair. Last night's amazing lovemaking came back in living color, but I forced my mind to move on. Thinking about *that* would just take away whatever edge I had. His chest also bore no mark and no obstruction for deflecting bullets or knives.

Thaddeus sniffed the air, like he was doing cocaine without the straw.

I frowned. "Are you on high drugs? Is that what this is all about? You're hallucinating?"

He grinned, rather wolf-like. "No, but I smell your arousal."

Ugh. T.M.I. No answer to that, I sat and stared at the top of his desk. What was my next move? *Damned if I know.*

"So, what do you want for lunch? You're my guest. I can't have you go hungry."

"You never let up, do you?" I shook my head. I was so far down the rabbit hole now that I swore I could see China.

"No. I've been told it's part of my charm."

"Fine. Whatever you're having." I might as well keep up my strength, at least until the calvary arrived. There was no way I wouldn't be missed when it was time for us to play our concert tonight, if not before. I just had to wait for this insanity to pass.

"Good. A drink in the meantime?"

"Why not? And could you button up your shirt? You've made your point."

"Oh, Miss Affini, as far as we've come already, I'm nowhere near finished making my point."

His words sent renewed chills slithering down my spine.

"What do you mean?"

"Aren't you one bit curious who it is that will fight for you at the challenge to be their lifelong mate?"

I didn't answer but shot him a disgusted look. Why should I care? It wasn't going to happen anyway.

"Unfortunately, I already have my Forever Mate. But our pack enforcer, and my right hand, Rocco? He wants you for his very own."

"You seem to forget we live in the twenty-first century. No woman has to put up with such things." I wrinkled my nose, reminding myself that these were idle threats. No way would Cristaldo go for this. *A multi-billionaire doesn't fight some kind of challenge for a woman. He just moves on and chooses another.* The thought did not make me feel any better.

"Ah, but you're more than just a woman. You're our future hope. Our fertility rates have plummeted alarmingly in recent years—not that they've ever been robust—but despite our best efforts, there's been too much inbreeding. You will help us change all that. You will be honored by all this...when you begin to understand your rightful place."

I rolled my eyes, unable to stop myself. *Humor him.* Soon the police or Cristaldo would arrive and he'd have to let me go. *Right?*

Chapter Seventeen

Cristaldo

"I'll do the talking." I stomped down the hotel hallway one step ahead of Serge. I had insisted on coming. I wanted to look into their eyes and smell the truth on their skins.

I knocked loudly and the door rattled. It was opened instantly and I found myself staring at two wide-eyed females, one brandishing an umbrella.

"I need to speak to both of you about your friend, Everly."

"What about her?" Cleo asked, her eyes narrowing with suspicion. The one called Layla still held the umbrella, looking undecided.

"She left the hotel today and I'm worried about her running into trouble." I glanced at the umbrella and gave a slight shake of my head. *Like that will stop me.*

"We're only wanting some information," Serge said, obviously trying to act the peacemaker. I scowled at him and gave him the nod that I had this.

"The only trouble our friend has is she needs some alone time," Cleo said. Her body language was belligerent and off-putting, but so far, she was telling the truth.

"Yes, she's fine. She just wanted to be a tourist today without people hovering over her and making her think she's a weak female. Everly can hold her own. She's amazing with her ability to throw knives," Layla said, setting the umbrella down. Her tone had an edge of warning as well.

"She may think she's fine, *you* may think she's fine, but there's a lot you don't know about this situation. She's in danger. I insist you tell me why she left and where she is. Has she texted you?"

"Yeah, danger, right!" Cleo scoffed. "You already cried wolf on that one."

The words cut to the chase and I gave her a quick look. Did she suspect something? No. Just a human expression.

"Be that as it may, Miss Affini needs to be found, and any information you can share would be greatly appreciated. Some fresh intel has made us somewhat concerned. About some concert goers that are a little too enamored of your friend, if you get my meaning?" Serge cut in again, earning a scowl from me.

"It did get a little crazy at the end of last night's concert, Cleo," Layla said, giving her friend a concerned look. "Maybe we should share what we know?"

"Right. Not sure I buy it. You already lied to her once," Cleo said, then clammed up. She hadn't wanted to say that much, that was clear. It was becoming more difficult to hold my wolf back from shaking all the truth out of the confounding women. I was the alpha and had the right to intel on any member of my pack...even if she didn't know she was a member yet. *But will be soon.*

"Is that what this is all about? She was upset with me?" I asked.

"Why shouldn't she be upset?" Layla said. "Everly's our friend, and you lied to her about Jason Stubbs being in town."

"How do you know that?" I didn't deny the charge. It was true, but I needed to know how this catastrophe had occurred and, somehow, I had to keep it from ever happening again.

"An RCMP officer — a Mountie — called. Told her she was safe. That Jason Stubbs is in jail and has been for days. So, why did you lie to her? To our friend?" Cleo said, her eyes filled with mistrust.

"Yeah, Everly will not put up with anyone lying to her, and *especially* not a man. Lie to her and it's your loss. You'll be eating her dust," Layla added from under arched eyebrows.

No one talked to me this way, but the harsh reality was that this had been all my doing. My mate going out unprotected had happened because I had wanted her safe with me and I hadn't been able to share with her the real reasons, owing to my need to protect my pack. But how could I have acted any differently, damn it? I didn't go in for self-doubt. *No alpha does.* But I could see the strategic error of my approach nevertheless.

"Did she give you any indication of where she was going today?" Serge asked.

"Not specifically. She's just going to walk around and do touristy things. One of the reasons why we wanted to come to Vegas," Layla said.

"Thank you for sharing what you know," Serge said, then gave me a nod.

He was right. There was no more intel to be had.

"Good day, ladies," I said and headed out the door.

"Wait, what about tonight's concert? Will there be more security?" Cleo asked.

I didn't wait to hear Serge's answer, but strode down the hallway. My cell phone rang, and I pulled it from my jacket pocket and checked the number. Why was Thaddeus calling?

"What do you want?"

"Seems Everly Affini has wandered into my casino today. Thought you might like to know that."

"What have you done?" I barked, and my wolf braced for action.

"Calm down. Just a little ploy to get her to come to us. I'm calling you as a favor. Something I'm certain we'd not have received if the event had occurred under *your* roof, Cristaldo."

Fucking politics and pack pride.

"Is she there with you? Let me speak to her. If you've harmed her in anyway—"

"She's here. And she's well. No need for dramatics."

I held the electronic device so tightly that the screen cracked under the strain.

"What do you want?"

"We know all the facts about the she-wolf's heritage. I'm calling to inform you that Rocco will be challenging you at the Lupercalia, which will be held at a neutral location that both packs agree upon. In the meantime, we will both have one of our own guarding her, so no one steps over the line. Is that amenable to you?"

His words pushed me to the limit. "I want to see her, and now, if you don't want a war on your hands."

"I'm too old and wise to want to fight a war over a female. Even one as rare as Miss Affini. I have my Forever Mate and she wants our pack to live in peace." Thaddeus sighed before continuing. "And for the sake of my mate and offspring, I will see this done the correct way, with a strict following of pack rules. Do you accept the challenge, Cristaldo Luceres?"

"I do. Now put her on the phone."

"Visiting hours will be set up. Both you and Rocco will share time with Miss Affini before the challenge. Of course, neither of you will be allowed to be alone with her without her permission. Acceptable?"

As long as my mate was kept away from Rocco, I was going to have to acknowledge the deal. *For now.*

"Yes, acceptable. What have you told her? Is she aware of who she is? And how in the hell did you find out?"

"No need for profanity. I have my methods. And yes, I've shared with Miss Affini the truth of her heritage. Not that she seems to believe as yet. That will take time. Send your second over and we will work out the arrangements."

Fuck. Did I have a traitor in my pack? Who had dared share the lab results? I hung up and called Lucius. "Come home. We have a situation."

I disconnected and realized Serge had joined me. He gave me a curious look, filled with concern.

"What's going on, sire?"

"House of Ribelle bullshit. I've called Lucius back home." I went on to explain the facts. Serge's eyes grew wider, but he waited for the full picture before speaking.

"This is about the best outcome we could have hoped for. Thaddeus will keep his word. He has more to lose than us if he doesn't handle this properly, with his finances stretched at the moment, not to mention a Forever Mate and a young pup. It keeps a shifter on track."

I snarled. "He'd better, or starting a war will be the least of his problems."

"We have another problem. How are we going to handle Everly's bandmates? We can't have them raise suspicions about her whereabouts. It will harm our pack, violate our code of secrecy."

"Right." Though I was fighting with my wolf not to storm the Ribelle Casino, tearing the throat out of anyone in my path, I had to handle this situation correctly and protect my pack, though every fiber of my being wanted to protect my mate first. "Let me think. Everly said she wanted space. What if she was so upset about the problems at last night's concert that she decided to take off on a road trip? We can use her phone to text the information."

"Yes, good thinking, sire. I'll advise Thaddeus of this."

"Find out where Everly will be staying. Demand a neutral location."

"Anything else, sire?"

"Yes, but I'll take care of it."

Chapter Eighteen

Everly

"What's going on? What did Cristaldo say?" I asked Thaddeus. My lunch sat cold and untouched, except for a couple of bites. Being kept in the dark was the worst experience of my life. And yeah, sitting across from a madman-slash-werewolf wasn't helping.

"Apparently you're going on a little road trip across our great county."

"What does that even mean?"

"It means that Cristaldo came up with a way to explain your absence so your friends will not alert the authorities." He took another swig of his wine, having already cleaned his plate so not one crumb remained. I almost expected to see him lick it clean.

"Cristaldo lied to my friends?"

"He was not given much choice on the matter. We can't have the police descending on us and discovering who we really are. We keep our pack safe by following

Rule One—*The existence of our kind must never be revealed.* Keep that in mind, Miss Affini. Loose lips means you lose them."

I absently licked my lips, disliking the disgusting threat with every fiber of my being.

"How many pack rules are there?"

"A handful. But only number one must never be violated under penalty of death."

"I guess it worked. I've never believed in werewolves. No one does beyond the pages of books and legends."

"That's for the best. It's meant to protect you as well."

"Right. So you say," I said, unable to keep the scoffing tone from my voice.

He sighed. "It will take time for you to believe. But trust me, don't take too long. Many things are afoot and you will lose control of your situation even further if you fight the truth."

I had nothing to say to that. Cristaldo had lied again. To my friends this time.

"Hand me your phone."

"What?" I laid a protective hand on my phone. I had intended to use it soon as I had a moment alone. "No way. It's private."

"Hand it over or I shall be forced to take it from you. Your choice."

I sat and glared at him. His eyes bored into mine. He meant what he said.

"Fine." I took the phone from my pocket, entered my password to unlock the screen and tossed it across the desk. He caught the device with lightning-quick reflexes in mid-air. "But I need to use the ladies' room."

"As soon as we take care of this, I'll have you removed to more comfortable quarters."

I had to make one more attempt to end this charade. "Look, if you're as smart as you think you are, you would just let me go. I have no intention of passing on such an insane tale of werewolves in Vegas. Heck, no one would believe me anyway." I rolled my eyes.

Picking up my phone, he took a few minutes to read a few of my messages before his fingers began flying over the keyboard. "There, that will finish things. They won't expect a message from you for a while."

"Then you don't know my friends."

Ding.

I raised my eyebrows at him.

He frowned, reading the text. "Young people today," he muttered and began to compose another text.

"They'll never leave this alone. They know me too well. I'd never abandon them or the band and just head off into the sunset." I shook my head. "I'm not that selfish."

"Then you'd better figure out a way to persuade them or they will be dealt with."

My heart felt like it had been slammed with a huge hammer as his meaning hit. I bent over in pain, one hand pressed to my chest. "You can't mean that."

"People disappear in Vegas all the time. Muggings and crimes are at an all-time high. It's in their best interests to be persuaded you've had an epiphany and taken to the open roads." He stated it in such a calm manner that it impacted all the more.

"Hand it over," I demanded.

I took the phone with trembling fingers and read the messages. He'd even managed to sound like me in the texts, but it wouldn't be enough to stop them in their tracks. What would work? I wracked my brain while his eyes bored holes in my flesh.

I beg you not to question my decision. Everything is crowding me in – Jason Stubbs, the crazy concertgoers last night, Cristaldo's lying. I'm sorry. I never meant for this to happen. Please forgive me. I can't be in touch for a while. Love you forever, E. xxoo

Love you forever would tell them it was me.

Closing my eyes against the sudden rush of overwhelming pain, I swallowed the bile rising in my throat and hit Send. Would I ever see my friends again? And what about my family? I angrily blinked away the tears that stung my eyes. No way would I allow Thaddeus to see me weak. He'd never respect that.

"It's done." I set the phone back on the desk, making myself stay in the present and not wallow in my grief. "Now what?"

"Excellent. You will be our guest here, of course. Surrounded by luxury."

"A gilded cage is still a cage." I leveled a fiery glance at him. This time he had the grace to look away.

"This part will soon be over. Then you can run your own household as you see fit. My mate is particularly good at seeing all my needs are provided for." His lips quirked upward with satisfaction.

This was too much to take. "Goody for you."

He scowled. "You will not scoff at this life."

"Another one of your rules with penalty of what? Losing a limb? An eye for an eye bullshit?"

"Enough!" he barked.

I kept myself from flinching with difficulty. The guy was psycho to the nines. Maybe Cristaldo had had a point when he'd warned me about going out alone. But dear God, couldn't he have been honest and told me why?

Thaddeus answered his phone. A grunted conversation followed that I ignored, until he called my name.

"Change of plans. You will be housed at a neutral location. You'll be taken through the tunnels."

The door opened and in trooped the loathsome bodyguards that had corralled me into this dicey situation in the first place.

"Get up," the one called Rocco demanded. "And don't try anything, if you know what's good for you, or your friends. No talking."

"Good day, Miss Affini," Thaddeus said with a polite nod.

I was hustled out of the room and into the corridor, then down two flights of stairs, the men still controlling my every step. I was really beginning to *really* dislike the Ribelle crew. At the bottom, we turned right and marched down what must have been the underground tunnel Thaddeus had mentioned.

"Where are you taking me?"

No one spoke and I had no choice but to try to keep up with them with their longer strides and quicker movements. I stumbled after a few hundred yards and Rocco picked me up and continued to move onward down the endless tunnel, carrying me over his shoulder.

"Put me down, you psycho!" I screamed, beating on his back with my fists. It had no effect at all. I might as well have been patting him for all the interest he demonstrated. Then the creep had the nerve to smack my bottom with an open palm, hard enough to make me freeze, more in surprise than pain.

"You'll have your hands full with this one, Rocco, once you win the challenge," another of the crew stated in a smarmy tone.

"No woman gets the better of me. She will learn her place," Rocco said.

"You know *nothing* about women," I said, for all the women who had gone before me.

He remained silent this time but continued to stomp down the never-ending tunnel. I had no choice but to wait it out, blood rushing into my brain and pooling, making my head throb. None of this made any sense. Surely I would wake up and find it all a nightmare or hallucination? My mind spun with frightening thoughts, going round and round, and the scariest one of all was that I suspected I was wide awake.

Finally, the group began to climb a staircase. At the top, we continued for a short distance. From my vantage point, all I could see was a hallway carpeted in royal blue with gold trim. We stopped at an elevator and everyone squeezed on. Still hanging upside down, I couldn't observe the floor number that one of the men pushed.

When the elevator doors whooshed open, out we went. A quick swipe of a key card—judging by the beeping—and we entered a room.

Rocco set me on my feet and I swayed, dizzy from the dislocation. He steadied me, then waited for me to sweep my hair away from my face and tug down my clothing that had ridden up. I saw the moment he took note of my remaining three knives — a bit of respect replaced his continual scowl.

"Where am I?" I asked.

"In a neutral location. That's all you need to know."

"Now what happens?" I took a look around. *Definitely a gilded cage.* A high-end casino suite with sliding glass doors, lots of fancy chrome and plush white leather furnishings — at least it wasn't a dungeon.

"Now you wait."

"For what?"

He gave me an impatient look. "Didn't Thaddeus explain things well enough? Are you that dense?"

"Right. Like you're all a bunch of werewolves! Get a grip."

He snarled. "You need to learn respect. I can teach you that. Do you like to be disciplined?"

"Get the hell away from me."

"Your time will come. When I win, you will warm my bed, and learn to like it, Miss Affini." His expression did indeed appear wolfish.

I swallowed my fear, praying that Cristaldo would come. No way would he abandon me, not after what we had shared. The memory of his touch, his caresses, his body, filled me with desire. *Please, please don't abandon me.*

"Let's go."

The men left.

I stayed upright until the door closed behind them. Then I sank to the floor, my legs literally collapsing under me.

Chapter Nineteen

Cristaldo

The door to my office flew open and Lucius stormed in, his expression thunderous. I stopped my pacing and rushed to greet him.

He embraced me without a word in a tight hug that demonstrated his understanding, before pulling away.

"How could this have happened?" I asked. An intense rage filled me, threatening to spill over and endanger our world.

"We've grown too soft, thinking wealth is the ultimate goal. It's not. Connections to pack far outweigh it. And to keep us safe, we must instill fear and fight for what is ours, the twenty-first century be damned!"

"You will keep her safe?"

"You know that, brother."

We embraced again. I went to the wet bar and spilled three fingers of top-shelf whiskey into two glasses. "News?"

"Oh yeah, the Chameleon was spotted. Cleaned us out of a cool twenty thousand before she must have suspected they were onto her and got away. We'll catch her soon," Lucius said with confidence. I had no interest in the card counter at the moment and just took a gulp of the fragrant liquor.

"Has Serge firmed up the times?" Lucius asked, taking a swig of whiskey.

I nodded and checked the clock ticking too loudly on the mantelpiece, reminding me of every second my mate was not here. *With me. Where she belongs. Safe and protected.*

"My visit's in forty-seven minutes. At the Dragon casino. It was arranged by the House of Anche." The Anche pack had traditionally held a neutral position, their very name, Anchor, speaking of their belief in things being held to an even course. Also descended from ancient Roman heritage, they had split from the House of Ribelle centuries ago. At least *la mia bella donna* would be safe and well cared for in their hands.

Lucius drank the liquor in one large gulp. "I'll go now and meet you there."

"Thank you, brother."

"Just name your firstborn after me, that's all I ask."

"What is mine to give, you will have." I used our formal response and gave a nod, our pack's acknowledgment of owing a favor. Then the meaning of Lucius' words sank in as the door closed firmly behind him. Offspring, a child and a pup, created between us. My protective instincts flared again and my wolf, hungry for justice, made the air shimmer around me, wanting the change. *No. Stand down. Our time will come.*

* * * *

A noise in the hallway followed by a knock on the door of this luxurious but anonymous suite made me sit up with a start. I scrambled to my feet and went to the peephole. A man and a woman stood outside my room. Neither looked particularly threatening, though the man was large in size and at least two decades older than me. The woman was young and pretty and well attired in a short yellow dress.

What do I have to lose? I opened the door and confronted them.

"Miss Affini. May we come in?" the man asked in a formal manner. The young woman, about my age, smiled. They seemed harmless enough. Maybe they could help alert the authorities to my predicament? On second thoughts, they knew my name, so they were probably in on it.

"Why not?" I waved my hand at them to enter. "You should know I'm being held here against my will."

The man ignored my words, confirming my suspicions, and shut the door. "I'm Leonardo, and this is Ember Rose, my daughter."

"What do you know about what's going on?" I demanded.

"I know enough that you need to calm yourself." He shook his head. "We are offering you sanctuary. A place of neutrality until things are resolved."

"Things are resolved!" My anger flared. Who the hell did these people think they were? It wasn't all nicey-nicey, being snatched and told my abductors were freakin' werewolves.

"I know you must have loads of questions," Ember Rose said. "I've come to help you. I can explain how things work for our packs. I understand you're a rare find, Everly. You must be proud. Wow! First dual breed in a hundred years. Amazing you've come to us." Her eyes shone with an excess of emotion, confusing me all the more.

"Will you be staying with me for a while?" I asked, curious as to her role in all this, even while my anger simmered. At least I could maybe get some sane answers.

"Why does everything have to come to a head during the lead-up to a blood moon?" Leonardo asked, looking up from his phone with a loud sigh. "You'll have to excuse me, Miss Affini. Business calls." He kissed his daughter's cheek and cautioned, "Be careful and follow all the rules," before leaving us alone.

"Well, this is nice." Ember Rose, Little Miss Sunshine, skipped over to the far side of the room and drew the drapes, exposing a huge bank of windows. "Oh, we can see right across Vegas."

"Excuse me if I'm not quite as excited as you. But I've had a nightmare day. Some psycho kidnapped me and told me I'm a werewolf. Oh, and he's one too."

"Hmm. Yeah, I can see your perspective. But have no fear. You're going to *love* being a wolf. It's awesome to be able to do what we can do." She ticked her points off on her fingers. "Superhuman strength and movement, night vision, great hearing, quick healing, longer life, the Lupercalia festival, alphas fighting to claim us, and don't get me started on about how we mate when we're claimed. Oh boy, wait until you find out about *that*." She rolled her eyes, her expression ecstatic.

"Stop right there. You think you're a werewolf?" My voice rose three octaves.

"Well, I am. Want to see?"

"Ah — yeah." This should be golden. I couldn't hold back my smirk. At least Ember Rose was going to prove entertaining.

"Just don't move, okay? Not for any reason," she warned.

I nodded. "Fine."

Strange refractions of light, almost a shimmering, made the air around me become suddenly visible. Prism rays of sky blue and white shot outward. A human-sized breach, like a portal that glimmered, revealed a glimpse into another dimension right next to ours. Scientists talked of eleven dimensions, a fact that boggled my mind, but what happened next blew me away totally and I knew I would never, *ever* see the world the same again. For in a blink of an eye, Ember Rose disappeared, only for something else to appear in her place. Something that should not have been there. A giant wolf, gray with amber eyes.

I stood absolutely still, not daring to breathe or move a single damn muscle. Had I totally lost all my marbles...or was a wolf actually advancing toward me, tongue lolling? Frozen in fear, I watched it come closer. And closer. Closer still. When its huge head banged against my shoulder, it was all I could do not to run screaming and smash the glass right out of the window in my panic. In my mind's eye, I imagined myself tumbling to the street below, a wolf clamped to my flesh.

Then the reverse happened. A shimmer of light, a sense of another place, another time, and Ember Rose reappeared. She grinned at me. "Cool, right?"

I dared to breath and tried to find my footing. I would have sworn the ground beneath my feet trembled and pitched as if from a real-life earthquake, except that Ember Rose wasn't reacting. "That was *something*."

"Glad you didn't move. It's awesome to see the first time. But you took it well." She turned her head sideways and gave me a long, level look. "Really well."

"You have no idea what just went through my mind."

"You'll enjoy the change — well, after you get used to the sensation. It can make you a bit seasick the first few times."

"I'll bet." My mind had seized. When would I wake up from this nightmare? *It has to be a dream, right?*

"Your first challenger, Cristaldo Luceres, that awesome alpha hottie, will be arriving in an hour. Though his twin, Lucius, *oh my God*, is to die for! And could you just imagine taking on the two of them? Or their twin brothers, Alessandro and Maximus! It's rumored *they* favor one mate...shared between them." She waved a hand in front of her face to fan herself. "Anyway, let's get you cleaned up and looking presentable. You don't want to meet your possible future mate looking less than your best." Her voice seemed far away, as though she was still in the other place she'd just shifted from.

"Yeah, right."

I let her lead me to the bathroom. "You get showered and I'll check out the closet."

"Sure." I turned on the shower full blast, stepped in and let the hard, driving rivulets hit my head and shoulders. What the heck had just happened?

When a knock on the door sounded a little later, I turned off the water and dried myself, then threw another towel around my dripping hair. I used the blow dryer Ember Rose had thoughtfully set on the vanity along with a tray of brand-new cosmetics, and put on a white robe before opening the bathroom door.

"There you are. Oh dear, you forgot makeup. We need to fix that. Sit. I *love* applying makeup. One of my favorite pastimes." She gestured at the vanity seat in front of the sink.

"Of course."

She gave me a glance. "You're in shock. Perfectly understandable."

She went to work on me, not stopping until she stepped back with a nod. "You are so lucky. Those cheekbones are to die for. And your eyes, such an amazing shade of green."

"Thanks."

"What color of lipstick would you like? I think red would be perfect."

"Whatever you chose is fine."

I waited while she set to work on my lips like she was painting the Mona Lisa from scratch. "There. Take a look."

I swung my head around to look in the bathroom mirror. She had done a great job—too bad I was too disconcerted to really appreciate it.

"Thanks. You've very good."

She smiled. "We're going to be besties. I just know it." Then she turned serious. "I should explain a few more things before Cristaldo arrives."

"Fire away." What else could I learn that would be any crazier than seeing her shift into a gray wolf? But again, I was wrong. In the next ten minutes I learned more than enough to send me to a psych ward for life. It was forbidden to consult with witches — they were universally hated by werewolves due to some old baggage about curses and hexes — and consort with other supernatural beings without permission. Oh, and vampires existed but preferred to keep their distance. The warnings about witches had been repeated *twice*, so they were pretty much the only bit of advice I considered important.

"Enough," I said, holding my hands up in defeat. "I don't want my head to explode."

A knock on the outside door made me jump.

"He's here. Get dressed. I'll stall him." Ember Rose closed the bathroom door after thrusting some clothes and shoes at me.

I quickly did as she asked, not wanting to get caught naked, pulling on the fresh underwear, short red number and stepping into the matching shoes she'd provided. Voices resounded through the door and seemed to be getting louder by the second.

Taking a deep, cleansing breath, I left the bathroom. Ember Rose noticed me straight away and gave me two thumbs up before exiting the suite, leaving Cristaldo to stand before me.

The air crackled between us. His dark gaze hungrily checked out every part of my body, then he locked eyes with me, as if he were seeking answers. He moved forward and enveloped me in a huge bear hug. "I thank the fates that you're okay," he murmured into my hair.

"I'm fine." My voice was muffled against his chest. I took a deep appreciative breath. His fragrance steadied me, making me more in control, more capable of dealing with things. This was instantly followed by throbbing desire centered deep inside me. I pressed my legs together, angry at my body for betraying my lust for this man.

"Why did you run from me, *bella*?"

His words broke the spell.

"I told you it was a deal breaker, lying to me. I know all about Jason Stubbs. You've been lying to me since the beginning about—about who you are." I pushed him away, unable to say the word *werewolf* and noticed there were three other men in the room. One was Lucius, and one looked familiar—maybe one of the bodyguards that had brought me here? And the third was Leonardo, back again.

"Miss Affini, you look lovely. My daughter, she's a marvel with the brush. Did you know she paints the most amazing watercolors?"

"No, she didn't mention it." Not that she hadn't told me a gazillion other things I wished I could forget. Though I had seen Ember Rose change into a wolf right before my eyes, a part of me still didn't believe it possible. I kept looking for a logical solution. A magic trick or sleight of hand. How could what I had seen be real?

I nodded at Lucius, my thoughts in turmoil.

"Miss Affini," Lucius said. As usual, he seemed to absorb most of the light in the room, his demeanor stiff.

"Who are you?" I asked, pointing at the third man.

"Rocco's second. Titus. Nice to make your acquaintance, royal miss," Titus said.

So polite. But under the surface ran a current of unease. My skin itched with odd sensations.

"They're here to make sure all that no one oversteps boundaries and follows pack rules. All for your benefit, Everly," Cristaldo explained.

Pack rules. The term suggested werewolf again. Oh hell, did that mean that every one of these men could shift into wolves like I'd seen Ember Rose do? Heat surged in my body.

"I need to sit." My vision was tunneling, fast.

Cristaldo swept me into his arms and deposited me on a sofa, sitting down close beside me, using one arm to hold me to his side.

"Get her a drink," he barked.

"Water," I croaked.

Lucius was the fastest and handed me a glass of cold water that I drank down greedily.

"Better?" Cristaldo asked, taking the glass from my hands.

"Yes, thank you."

"Good," he said gently, tucking a strand of hair back from my face.

He smiled, a genuine smile, and I caught a glimpse of the man under the surface. It was too bad I couldn't trust him, because he had a good heart and really did care about his family. And how was that different from my own way of thinking? I'd do most anything for family. *But we're not saying we're freakin' werewolves and thinking that explains the insane things we do running roughshod over others.* Confused didn't begin to cover this situation. Nothing in the world could have prepared anyone for this, I was certain of it.

"Now, the rules allow you two to go off by yourselves into another room, if both parties consent. But be warned, if anything untoward occurs, the penalty is severe. Your personal fortune is surrendered to the other house and you must step down as alpha, the taking of the life of the instigator of the crime to be voted on by all pack members in the houses affected," Leonardo explained, as though he was discussing the weather. None of it made any sense.

The trio of men settled down at a good distance in front of the television set and began to watch some sports, turning up the volume.

"So, Thaddeus shared some odd history with me earlier," I ventured.

"Yes. I was informed." A shadow crossed over his handsome face.

"You know it all sounds crazy, right?"

He stroked my cheek. "We can't help who we are. Who we are born to be, my beautiful Everly."

His words startled me, with their calm acceptance of the way things were, making the whole situation far more real. *Okay. Maybe* werewolves existed. And if they did, then...other things...might happen too.

"So, what's the deal with this challenge thing everyone keeps mentioning? And the Lupercalia?"

"It means I fight Rocco to be your Forever Mate." His tone might have been neutral, but the words were not.

"Fight? Like, men kickboxing? In a ring?" The thought of two men fighting over me made my head ache.

"No. Fight as wolves in a pit."

"What? That's insane! With all your money and power and position, you still do crap like that? In this century?" I couldn't comprehend it. I certainly didn't want Cristaldo to get hurt on my account. Even if he had lied, he didn't deserve this. I had to do something, *anything*, to avoid that happening.

"It's what we do."

"No! I absolutely forbid it. I don't want anything to happen to you." In my mind's eye, I could see him wounded in a terrible battle. Intense anger followed on the heels of fear. My body felt foreign, my hands curling so tightly into my palms that the pain grounded me.

"I won't, *bella*. I'm stronger than Rocco and far more skilled. We're the chosen ones and will be Forever Mates. Trust me. This is the way."

"Trust you? But you've lied to me before." I ignored the 'Forever Mates' tag. *Later.* After I'd said my piece.

"Only to keep you safe. I am compelled to protect my mate. I can't help it."

"Where is it written you have to lie to protect someone? I could have handled the truth."

"The truth. You say that now, but how about days ago? Would you have understood that I was a werewolf that wanted you for his mate? Can you honestly say you wouldn't have run away?"

It sounded so ludicrous spoken aloud. "I don't know. But I can't do a relationship — if this is where this is headed — based on lies. I just can't do that. You must trust me when I say I can handle the truth. For heaven's sake, look what I handled today. You got me believing in werewolves. That I'm going to be one. I think I may need to see that in you — see you as a wolf — before I can truly believe that you are one, too." No matter how many times I said those words, it would never seem possible. I rubbed at my forehead, trying to ease my fevered mind.

"My first instinct is to protect. I know no other way. I can't change who I am, even for you. I can show you my wolf, if that will help you? But let's not waste a moment of this precious time together." He gently grasped my chin, tilted my face and pressed his fine lips to mine in a deep, soul-binding kiss that blocked out everything else. Locked together, our bodies entwined, an image of a wolf came to me, so real I swear that when I reached out a hand to stroke it, I touched thick gray-brown fur. The springy silkiness slipped through my nerveless fingers, emitting a clean, spicy fragrance that enticed my nose and my body. I breathed deeply, finding excitement and comfort in the sensation.

I squirmed, remembering we had an audience. "Let's go to the bedroom," I whispered against his mouth, our breaths intermingling. We needed time alone to sort this out.

Cristaldo swept me up into his arms and bore me to a bedroom, slamming the door shut with his foot.

A loud knock followed and Leonardo poked his head in. "Do you both consent?"

Cristaldo swore in Italian while I answered for both of us, understanding it was my approval that was required. "We do."

The door closed behind him and we were alone.

He came forward and embraced me. "I want *you*. Like the earth needs the sun's rays, I need your touch, your light. Say you want me too. I have no power against this pull — this need for you. I want you, Everly Affini, with me, always."

My body thrummed with need as well. I wanted this man in ways I could not have imagined twenty-four hours ago, but I didn't want to give him the wrong impression.

"It's not that I don't want you — I do. But I don't want you thinking this can be anything more than physical if we don't settle how things will work between us. I have a terrible track record with relationships. I've shown bad judgment in the past. I don't want that to happen again."

"I want more as well." His expression burned with intensity and an honesty that made me listen with care. "I want to have all of you. Physical, spiritual and mental. I don't want you for a day, or a week—I want you for life. We can work this out and be what the other needs. Our journey is written in the stars. Give us that chance."

His words gave me hope. "I want you too. Since I first saw you, I've thought of nothing else." I could be honest as well, let the barrier drop. *For now.*

He leaned in and kissed me with a solemnity that stirred my soul. I returned his kiss. Sensations rose from inside me, a raging tornado of lust surging to the surface.

Our kiss turned desperate as he slammed me up against the wall and tore the dress from my body in one quick movement. I pushed his suit jacket over his shoulders and yanked the buttons off his shirt to feel his bare skin against mine. I unzipped his pants, and he kicked them to the side.

He grabbed my bra and tore it off, and my panties followed, ripped to shreds. I tugged down his briefs, and his cock sprang free. Solid and, *oh*, so fine, precum glistening at the wide, inviting tip.

He threw me onto the bed. His hungry gaze stroked down the length of my body, drinking me in like an alcoholic parched for sustenance.

"So beautiful," he murmured.

The heat simmered between us, the air a living thing. I would never as long as I lived forget the way he looked at me then, his eyes seeing only me. It lit a fire inside me and I wanted him to look at me like that always, as though I was the most important person in his universe.

He lifted my legs wide and knelt between them. I muffled my screams with a hand as he used his talented mouth to capture my pussy, applying his thick, strong tongue to lick the length of my sensitive folds, swiping right through me. He found my clit and rolled it between his lips, sucking, balancing me precariously on the threshold of an orgasm. My pussy quivered with the need for release, more urgent by the second.

"Don't stop. Please, *please* keep going, I'm — *ahh* — almost there," I said. Cristaldo knew how to touch a woman. Everything was magnified with him, to the point where soon even his blazing stare might make me orgasm.

"Wait for me. I want you to come on my cock."

He placed my legs over his shoulders and slid his thick cock through my swollen flesh, in and out, the rhythm hard and fast. My body shook with each push and my muscles rippled around his shaft, milking him, drawing him in tighter.

"You taste of heaven. So wet and tight for me. Take it all, baby. I've been waiting my whole life to find you." He thrust into me harder and it was all I could do to hold on. I was adrift on a sea of lust. An urgent need for release made me tilt my hips to meet his every stroke.

"Make love to me like there's no tomorrow, Cristaldo. Like I'm the last woman on earth." *Like it's the last time ever.* Because I would do anything for this man, even if it killed me.

He slammed into me harder, pushing my legs farther apart, and I lost all coherent thought. "Oh, baby," I whimpered as he used his teeth to graze my neck, circling my clit with one thumb. I shuddered, and he grabbed my face and brought it to his.

"Look at me when I fuck you," he commanded. The change in position claimed something more inside me, and I convulsed when he pushed deeper. His body pistoned mine in a wild tempo, and I gripped his arms, staring up at him, our eyes locked.

Then he stopped and withdrew his cock. I mewled aloud, protesting the lack of warmth and the unwanted sensation of emptiness. But then I was swept over onto my knees in one quick motion, my thighs wide apart, and he was mounting me from behind. He reached down with one hand and rubbed my throbbing clit, squeezing and pinching. When he swatted my aching pussy a couple of times, I let loose a moan. In the throes of an alarming desire, I was pushed further than I had ever imagined possible.

"Yield to me," he growled, spanking my pussy again, light slaps that pushed me over the edge.

I was so vulnerable in this position, with his huge body grinding into mine. The pleasure and pain took my mind away from the fullness I was now experiencing. The position seemed to have opened me up too far, and I struggled to take all of him.

He was so hard, so swollen, and I nearly lost consciousness with how overwhelming it was. Suddenly he was impossibly tight within me and it felt incredible. I had no idea where he began and I ended. Each little movement was magnified. We were one, our bodies taking us further than our minds ever could.

"Holy fates," he shouted. He let loose a howl that stormed through me, electrifying every cell, and the hot cum flooded my pussy, heating me to the core.

I went over the edge with him, my orgasm sending shockwaves throughout my body for long, precious moments afterward. This wasn't sex—this was an apocalyptic event.

I'm ruined.

Chapter Twenty

Cristaldo

My Everly lay contented in my arms, her body twined around mine, her flesh hot and flushed from our lovemaking. I pressed kisses to her smooth forehead, my breath slowly returning to normal. I had been so close to knotting with her fully, but some sense of control had remained.

Surely she could see what was now so obvious, that we were perfect for each other? What was a lie or two to protect her or my pack? But when she looked at me with those huge green firelit eyes, as though she could see right through me, I swear I wished it were different. That I could be all that she wanted me to be. Be the upstanding man of her dreams, my life not bound by pack demands.

"What happens now? Am I stuck here until the event? And then what—can I choose to go home? Because I swear to God, if you try to keep me here, I will run." She stabbed me with a finger in the chest with each word. I grabbed her hand and held in it mine while she continued her rant. "Every chance I get. No one boxes me in. Even a werewolf. No matter how awesome the sex is. And it was great, by the way. Better than great. The best. Just so you know."

I swallowed my anger and my need to rebuke her. To thrust her back into line like an alpha is sworn to do. She had acknowledged our connection. How good we were together. My wolf was winning, making him content for the moment.

"You stay in this room until the night of the full moon—tomorrow. Then you'll be brought to the fight as witness to my winning. Then no one will ever harm you again. You'll be under my protection and the protection of the House of Luceres until the day you leave this Earth."

"What if I go back to Canada?"

"Why would you want to do that? You'd be Nomad. A wolf alone, vulnerable to moon sickness. You would never be happy living with only humans. Your wolf nature is rising here in Vegas, so close to the magic. It's in your eyes. I see it. Yes, of course you can visit your family. Just don't live with them full time. It's dangerous for you, for them, *la mia bella ragazza dolce.*"

"Don't call me that."

"See, the anger you feel—it's your wolf calling. It's growing stronger by the hour. Soon you won't be able to control it without training. I can offer you that. The finest training there is."

"What if I don't want to become a werewolf?"

I snarled and fear mixed with the anger in her eyes. She turned a defiant jaw to me, her lips pressed firmly together. Only for her would I ignore the disrespect.

"Would it be so bad? Being here with me? Becoming a wolf is only part of who you would be. Most of the time you'd be exactly who you are now, just with powerful benefits."

"And that benefit includes lying about things? Keeping things hidden from the outside world?"

"I didn't lie because I wanted to. I lied to you before because I *had* to, because I *must* protect my pack." I raked a hand through my hair. "Why are we going over this again? I thought you understood?"

"No matter how you try to tell yourself that, I don't believe you can't do it differently. My last boyfriend — and don't growl, it doesn't become you — was a pathological liar. Thank heaven he's in jail. But I won't do it again — the doubts, the mistrust... My lover must be able to trust me one hundred percent, and I need that from him as well."

I wanted to spill it all that once I claimed and marked her, she was mine. That all choice would be taken away. My lips actually opened of their own accord before a loud knock at the door clamped them shut again. Now I would never know what I was going to say. Whether I could trust Everly, or myself, enough to spill my secrets.

"Sorry, but your time's up, brother," Lucius said, his voice surprisingly diffident through the barrier.

"We'll be out shortly," I said, managing to keep my wolf in check. How much longer I could keep him under control was another matter. My body ached from the power required to hold him at bay and allow me to leave her. "I have to go, *tesoro*. But I will see you at the challenge."

"Not before?" Her voice sounded afraid for me and I rushed to reassure her, even though her concern made me proud. She cared more than she knew, far more than simply the lust of discovering great sex with the perfect partner.

"I will win. Have no fear of that."

"No! I don't want you doing that! No fighting over me. I forbid it!"

"It's not up to you, *bella*." I took her hand and caressed the soft skin on her inner wrist. It soothed her enough that she became quiet.

She remained subdued as I dressed her in fresh clothes I found in the closet, to replace those I'd torn from her. Then I dressed, ignoring the torn shirt, and buttoned up my jacket.

"Will I turn soon? You know, find my wolf?" She frowned as she asked, chewing on her bottom lip.

"You might. Or it might not be until you've been mentored and assisted with the transformation."

"What if it happens while you're not here?"

"No fear of that."

"Why not?"

"You're being influenced by me right now. That's why your wolf is rising to the surface. It's calling out to mine. Our wolves are chosen to be mated, same as the human side. It goes in tandem. That's why we're called Forever Mates."

She ran a hand through her hair, tugging hard at the roots. "It's all so complicated and hard to understand when you haven't been raised in a pack. I'm just coming into all this and you were born to it. Part of me still doesn't really believe it."

"Believe it. Give yourself time. I promise, it will get easier."

"But if we're destined mates, why is anyone challenging that?"

"You're more special than most. You could be mated to another house. That's your dual breed nature, since our houses splintered apart. Your bloodline is ancient — you come from the original wolf."

"But I'm not anyone else's Forever Mate, right?"

"No. But you could still have offspring with another house, which is why they want you. Mainly for breeding purposes, which demands I fight and win."

"*Yuck*. What if I don't want children?"

"Do you want children, Everly?" This was important, important enough that I had to look deep into her eyes to see the truth of it.

"Well, yes, just not right this *exact* second. I mean, I'd prefer to be married first — to the man of my choosing, maybe with a house paid for?"

Relief filled me. What if she had said no? It would have been such a loss. But she had said *yes* and my wolf leapt for joy.

"I want children. As many as possible. I'm stating that right up front."

"Aren't you getting ahead of yourself?" She stood her ground, one of those things I found most maddening and yet so endearing. I wanted a strong mate, not a pushover, but I wanted her to be able to follow my lead when it mattered. *To protect her.*

Another knock came.

"I do hate to interrupt, but you've gone past your allotted time by an hour," Leonardo called through the closed door, his respectful tone tinged with anxiety.

"I'll see you tomorrow." I leaned down and pulled her tightly against me, kissing her like I never wanted her to go. "I'm falling for you, Everly," I whispered in her ear. "We can build a life on that."

She said nothing, her body stilling. When I moved from her side and looked back, the worry and concern for the future was obvious in her brilliant green eyes. I wanted to stay with her, reassure her all would be well. But I held my head high and forced myself to leave. *Soon, my love, we will be together forever.*

I have to get away. Find a way to leave. Not only to keep my transformation at bay — he'd admitted that he was the one influencing me to want to change and that the land Vegas was built on had a powerful pull of its own — but mostly to prevent Cristaldo from fighting over me and getting hurt. *Or worse.* I could *never* allow that to happen. *But how?*

My mind raced in circles, looking for an idea even as I watched Cristaldo walk out, his expression and body language tense. When the suite went silent, I ventured forth and found it empty. *Good.* I hurried to peek out through the peephole and found Lucius and the one called Titus guarding both sides of the doorway. *Damn.* I wouldn't be getting out that way.

I needed to sneak out under their very noses. My stomach rumbled, reminding me that I hadn't eaten lunch. *Yes.* It could work.

Picking up the phone, I ordered a number of dishes from the restaurant. While I waited, I retrieved my remaining knives. After showering, I changed into pants and a simple white blouse. I strapped the belt that held my weapons around my waist and added a long black jacket to hide them. Retrieving my wallet from my carryall, I slid it into my pants pocket. I added a couple of changes of underwear as an afterthought, then pulled my hair into a secure ponytail. I gave a quick glance in the mirror and, satisfied with my preparations, sat down on the bed to wait.

A loud knock on the door and I jumped to my feet. *Now for the hard part.* The door opened and the waiter swept in, pushing a large serving table covered by a flowing white tablecloth, just like I had prayed for.

"Where do you want it, miss?" he asked.

"In the bedroom."

I smiled at the two men in the doorway. "Would you like something to eat?"

Lucius shrugged. "Nothing for me. We ate during the game. While you were—busy." He raised his eyebrows with a speculative look, reminding me so much of his brother and why I was doing this. Or at least trying to. *Please, please make it work.*

Titus shook his head.

I turned and followed the waiter into the bedroom. He pushed the cart up close to the bed.

"Will that work for you?" he asked. He was quite young, eager to please, like a college student working for his tuition. I might make this happen, but I would need all my powers of persuasion.

"Maybe over in that corner?" I pointed. Yes, definitely out of sight of the doorway.

He did as I asked. "Better?"

Reaching under my jacket, I slowly withdrew a knife. God, I hated to do it, but I was backed into a tight spot, with no other viable choice that I could see.

When he saw what I was brandishing, his eyes grew two sizes larger. My heart sank at the fear obvious in his stare.

"Don't say anything, please. I promise, I won't hurt you. I just need you to listen to me. Okay?"

He nodded.

"I have to get out of here. I'm being held against my will by those two men outside. I want you to hide me under that tablecloth, push me out of here and take me to the kitchen. Can you do that for me? Do you understand? I've been kidnapped. I don't want to be here." I whispered as quietly as I could. I only had a few seconds to convince him of my desperate situation.

He nodded again, his Adam's apple bobbling up and down, his eyes filled with understanding. "I can do that."

I bent down, picked up the edge of the table linen and found what I was looking for — a steel shelf just big enough to hide me. For once I was glad to be small-boned, though I had been bullied growing up, teased about my pint-sized appearance. This had been part of the reason I'd become a drummer — I could make a lot of noise and yet hide in the background.

"Help me put these dishes on the dresser," I said and grabbed the silver-covered plates to begin transferring them over. He did as I asked, his face white as a sheet. I gave this plan a fifty-fifty chance of working. But what else could I do but try?

"One last thing." I snatched up the pepper mill. "Please sprinkle this on me."

His eyes widened at my request, but he gamely went ahead and twisted the tall silver cannister over me. I held my nose to keep from sneezing. *Let this be enough to keep them from noticing.*

"Please don't say anything. My life depends on it." I climbed onto the lower shelf of the cart and pulled the cloth downward to straighten it.

"Okay, go," I said.

The cart began to move. A lump tightened in my throat. I prayed like I had never prayed before. *I'll never ask for anything from you again as long as I live. But don't let them check.*

Chapter Twenty-One

Everly

Being blinded by the tablecloth that covered the cart made ghostly images move in and out of my field of vision. Nervous perspiration broke out all over my body. Could they not hear my heart pounding? So much rode on these next few precious minutes. I blinked rapidly at the sweat dripping and stinging my eyes, not daring to move a muscle or even breathe.

"Add a generous tip for yourself. Hey, that steak must have been over-peppered," Lucius said, giving a sharp sneeze. He sounded so close that I swore I could reach out and touch him. There was no point in using a knife against my bodyguards after Thaddeus' powerful demonstration of its ineffectiveness. But the waiter, I was fairly certain, was human. He didn't have the imposing power of the wolves, and he seemed to care that I was in trouble. *If only his nerves withstand the test...*

The cart lurched out into the hallway.

"You'd better start working out with weights, buddy, that cart's giving you some trouble," Lucius said, the smirk obvious by his tone.

"Just a bad wheel needs replacing," the waiter said, his voice high-pitched from the strain. *Hold it together, buddy.* I licked the salt dripping onto my lips. *Just get me to the elevator.* I could take it from there.

As the cart creaked down the hallway, its wheels began spinning faster and faster. *Don't draw too much attention.*

I heard the *ding* of the elevator opening, then felt the lurch from going over the divide between the two separate spaces. *Just a few more seconds. Please.*

I waited in the semi-dark, my breath harsh, breathing through my mouth and counted the seconds that were passing with the consistency of molasses. My entire being was zeroed in on that one thing.

With a soft *whoosh*, the doors started to close. I faced the opening, aware of every nuance, and waited. It was the longest damn wait of my life.

When the elevator began to descend, I almost fainted, my whole body wobbly. I reached out and held on to the steel legs to brace myself.

"You can come out now." He lifted the tablecloth and peered down at me.

"Thank you," I croaked.

He gave me a hand and I crawled out. My limbs slowly unfolded as I stood upright—I had held myself so rigid.

"This elevator goes down to the basement and connects with the car park. Here's my keys. It's the red Ford Escort, in the staff parking area. Nothing special, but it works."

"I can't take your vehicle," I said.

"It's okay. Pay me back when you can." He pulled out a pad and pen and scribbled something. "This is my name and number."

"You should leave this place," I said, taking the piece of paper and shoving it into my pocket. "If they find out what you did, you'll likely be in trouble."

"I'm out of here today, anyway. I've always thought this place was off. Just didn't realize how far off. School starts in a few days. I'll be fine."

I was fairly certain he didn't know the full deal, that my kidnappers were werewolves. How could he? He was just a kid saving to go to college.

"Thank you. You're a lifesaver." I impulsively kissed his cheek.

He blushed brick red. "I'd do the same for my little sister."

The elevator doors dinged again and I stepped off. Nervous as hell, I ran as fast as I could to the area he'd pointed out, where the staff parked. A feeling of red laser dots boring into my back didn't help—I had to quit watching thriller movies that had guns poised ready to shoot someone fleeing a crime scene. Once I was away from the guy who'd helped me, I couldn't stop myself from worrying. He'd seemed too good to be true. What if he'd been a spy, planted by one of them?

The Ford Escort was so old that I had to use an actual key to unlock the driver's door. After a couple of attempts that failed because my hands were shaking so badly, I got it right and jumped into the driver's seat. My first attempt to turn the engine over failed. *Start. Please.* I held my breath, pumped the gas and gave a second try. It sprang to life.

Letting out a panicky breath, I put the transmission in reverse and backed out of the tight spot. Jamming it into drive, I set a course to the exit, keeping a sharp eye out for company.

When I was waved onto the street after the attendant noticed the staff card attached to the upper left windscreen, I turned left, heading away from the Strip.

But every mile I drove was one more away from Cristaldo, and each one made my heart ache more. I had it bad, my vision aching and blurry from unshed tears. But it was for the best. *For him. And for me.*

I had to get off this interstate. Thank heaven, the sign for a rest area lay dead ahead. I made a sharp right and drove onto the paved area. I left the car idle and cried with the pain of loss for who I'd thought I was. For how things would be from now on. And for having left a large part of myself behind in Vegas.

When I could cry no more, I sat back in my seat and stared at the landscape with bleak, wet eyes. I swiped at my nose with the sleeve of my jacket. *Where to go?* I couldn't chance going home, though I wanted nothing more than to climb into my mother's loving arms. I couldn't work in the States without a permit. I had my wallet with my credit cards, but that trail would be too easy to follow. How much cash did I have? I tugged it out to count. Three hundred and nineteen dollars, more than half in American money. Was that enough for gas and food to get across the border into Canada? It had to be. I'd sleep in the car if I had to.

Stiffening my spine, I placed the Escort in drive and entered the stream of traffic headed away from Vegas. The I-15 north should get me to Salt Lake City around midnight, where I could rest and eat something. I sighed, thinking of all the uneaten food left on the dresser back in the hotel room. It was going to be a long, cold night.

Chapter Twenty-Two

Cristaldo

"What the hell do you mean she's gone?" My wolf sprang to life. We both wanted to tear the hearts out of anyone standing in our way of finding her.

"I'm sorry, brother. She hid under the dining cart. I never thought anyone could fit under there, or would attempt such a risky move. She's got balls to go with those knives she carries. We found it abandoned in the parking garage, and the waiter's vanished as well. We left her alone to eat her meal and sleep, then when Leonardo and Rocco arrived this morning to see her, we found her missing."

The hardest choice of my life faced me — obligations to my pack versus bringing home my mate. Every cell in my body was torn asunder. Pain unlike any I've experienced before consumed me, ripping my heart in two. "You go. I've got to be there today. No choice," I croaked, my throat too tight with my wolf howling in disagreement. He wanted to track her down. *Now.* I fought him hard, but my hold was flimsy at best. I had no choice on that either. But later, when I unleashed his ferocious anger, then the die would be cast. *All debts settled.*

"You do what you have to, Cristaldo. I will find her and keep her safe for you."

Fuck. Why does it have to hurt so bad? "Keep me posted. Every hour on the hour without fail."

"Of course. I wish I could be there today for you, brother." He clapped me on the back.

"I'll ask Serge. I'm ready. The fates are behind this."

"Never doubted it for a second."

I glanced at my watch. I had just enough time to talk with Serge before we had to leave, when I would settle everything once and for all. I would fight for her, guaranteeing our path to be together. It was not the usual way of things. Most wolves would have stood down now, if their chosen mate had vanished. But I knew more than most. I had her close in my mind's eye, seeing all she saw, feeling all she felt.

* * * *

With each mile that passed, the pain grew. There seemed no end to it, a terrible sense of loss that darkened my soul. I pulled to the side of the road again, unable to drive through a veil of tears. I saw the truth of it now. Cristaldo had only lied to protect me, protect his pack. Yes, we would have to work on that, but it wasn't enough to stop our being together.

Damn. Tonight was the challenge and the Lupercalia. Such prideful events for the House of Luceres. And I had abandoned them, which now felt wrong on so many levels. Cristaldo wanted to fight for me, a simple, small-town girl, but one who came with an important heritage I had not fully embraced. One who came with gifts, I thought, remembering the amazing list that Ember Rose had shared. Would it be so bad? Could I pay the cost to be with him?

The thought surprised me, quickening something in me. Until now, all I had seen was the downside. Now I saw a clear path to helping others. A way to becoming so much more. A way to be with him.

Yes. When called upon, I had to step up. *You're not given anything more than you can handle, right?* At least I had to believe that, the survivors' creed.

And that damn moon was bothering me again. I scratched at my itchy skin. When I caught a glimpse of myself in the rear-view mirror, I jumped. My eyes had changed—luminous and bright blue, they glowed. I looked down at my hands holding the wheel. Claws were forming on the tips of my fingers. My whole body was tingling, changing, far more alive.

A vision formed in my mind. *Oh my God!* He wasn't stepping down from the challenge. My leaving had done no good. I had to get back!

My decision pushed all the pain away. I would drive straight through to be with him. Be there for the challenge. For the pack. But mostly for Cristaldo. It was my destiny. *Just please let me get back in time.*

I jerked the wheel of the Toyota to the left and made a quick, illegal U-turn, then gunned the engine of the vehicle with a hard press of my foot on the gas pedal, determined to head straight back to Vegas. Every second felt like an eternity as I focused only on driving, my whole body strained with worry. *Will I get there in time?* When I finally made the outskirts of the desert city, something beckoned to me in the darkness. A silverish light, like a path of energy, opened up. In a trance, I followed the ribbon-like trail down a series of roads into the desert.

Chapter Twenty-Three

Cristaldo

The blood moon overhead, I stood on the edge of the pit temporarily built in a remote spot in the desert for just this event, and glared across the space at my opponent. *Where is she?* Even as our connection grew tighter, she was not with us.

Leonardo's voice rang out loud and clear. "The Challenge of Cristaldo, Alpha of the House of Luceres and Rocco, Enforcer of the House of Ribelle will commence upon my signal. May the best wolf win the hand of the lovely Everly, daughter of the Affini family and the original wolf."

A loud bell rang out three times, signaling the beginning.

I closed my eyes and allowed the energy to flow through me. A loud shout came from the crowd when we both shifted to wolf, prepared to end this one way or another. A howl emanated from deep within my chest as I jumped ten feet into the pit and confronted the hated Ribelle enforcer.

We circled each other, looking for signs of weakness. I bared my fangs, keeping my body low. I had the advantage of being stronger and more driven to win than the cur that faced me. No one else would be with my mate. *Unthinkable.* I would kill first, tear the bastard to shreds. How dare he threaten me and my mate!

I launched myself at the enemy, slicing into his hip with extended claws as I attacked his flank. I had drawn first blood and the crowd howled their approval.

I kept him in my sights as we moved around the ring, stalking each other. When he launched himself at me, I was prepared. I jerked to one side and he swept by me, missing knocking into me by scant inches, though one of his claws raked my side. I ignored the small pain and focused on winning.

My actions were instinctive now, honed by many hours fighting in the ring with my pack brothers.

I watched carefully for him to make a misstep that would allow me to bite his vulnerable throat, to take him out. But he was an experienced fighter, one who knew enough to keep himself protected.

When I went for his throat, he ducked to the side at the last second. But I managed to catch his shoulder with my claws, drawing more blood. My thirst for the kill heightened at the sight of red flowing from his wounds and dripping onto the rocky soil. My vision tunneled until I could only see the devil wolf that wanted my mate.

End this, my wolf shouted, driving me forward.

The lust for blood and death overcame me. Dripping sweat and blood, I jumped on his back in a flash of movement so swift that the crowd went silent. I sank my teeth deep into the ruff on the back of his neck. I wanted to be a great fighter, like my father before me, a Luceres who had also been born on the night of the full moon, a Luceres who had nearly died for his Forever Mate.

The cur tried to shake me off, his great head and body bucking beneath me. I held on, driving my teeth in deeper, weakening my opponent. Then with a mighty twist of his spine, he threw me off and went for my throat.

He sank his teeth in close to my jugular, so close that my vision darkened with pain and fury. Then my mind exploded with the image of him and my mate making love, their bodies entwined beneath the gleaming moon. The putridness of it sickened and, more crucially, weakened me. *"Is it real? Did this happen? It can't be, can it?"* I called out to her and she answered.

"The dog tricked you. I would never betray you."

A loud gasp from the crowd drew the cur's attention. He let up on crushing my neck for one split second, but it was enough. I jerked away, blood springing from a gash in my neck. He'd managed to inflict a terrible wound and won by trickery and deceit, hallmarks of the Ribelle. I sent the hated image to Lucius to let him know the vileness of what had occurred. If I died this night, it must be known. *"It must be avenged, brother."*

A familiar and haunting scent caught my attention. A voice whispered on the wind and a presence solidified. I swung around in shock and fear to see Everly right in the ring with me. My spirit filled with the all-consuming need to protect her from this ugliness and danger, even as her presence blessed me with a few seconds to recover. But what was unbelievable was that she had shifted into a mighty she-wolf. Her eyes glared blue and her fur bristled, like the ancient wolves of Roman days. My heart stuttered at her being down here with our enemy, though it filled with joy at her wanting to be at my side. She had joined me, shown to one and all that she chose *me*.

"I wanted to defend us. To be by your side."

Her thoughts flew into my mind, as solid and real as if she had spoken them aloud. She stepped up and stood by me. Two against the world. The mongrel faced us for a moment, then lowered his head and lay down on his back, exposing his belly. I wanted to tear him to pieces, to sink my teeth into his flesh and pull him asunder, disgusted at the way he had tried to defeat me.

But I had won. We had won. *No need to kill him now.* Lucius was sharing what had occurred on the battlefield, explaining my mate's actions in having joined me. It was a breach of protocol, but one that should be excused with the extreme provocation Rocco had given us.

"Cristaldo, alpha of the House of Luceres, has won the challenge for his mate, Everly Affini of the original wolf. Let no man or wolf ever again contest his claim on his Forever Mate or her Forever Mate," Leonardo said, his voice ringing out loud and clear.

"You came. Defended us in the pit. Shifted for me." I stood in awe at her amazing actions. Never in the history of our houses had such a thing happened.

"I wanted to be at your side. Forever. I chose us."

We jumped out of the pit as a bonded pair to accept the congratulations of all the pack members that came forward to honor us and tender their respect. Our glorious victory would begin a new legacy for the House of Luceres, one built on blood and trust. But most of all built on love, for I loved my mate, through and through. And when she had leapt to my side in the heat of battle, she had cemented herself in our pack. This would be spoken of for years to come. She would become a legend in her own lifetime.

When we shifted back to human, I was already healing, my wounds closed and the pain easing.

I wanted to be alone with Everly now, to savor our victory, and I bore the final obligations of the ceremony with as much patience as I could muster. Then it was time for us to leave the reception, and I hurried my mate along the path that led to my helicopter. Now I could finish our courtship properly, mark her and make her one of ours.

The moon called louder at that second. My wolf surged just under the surface of my skin and I picked her up and bore her to my helicopter. Once she was buckled in, I got into the cockpit and prepared for take-off.

I set course for the closest open-space location I owned, a retreat high in the hills of Montana. "How does a hunting cabin with a hot tub and view from a mountaintop sound?" I queried.

"Perfect. If we're off the grid and all alone." Everly grinned.

I could promise that.

The wolf moon shone with all its ancient wisdom and seemed to point the way to our honeymoon destination. Or at least that was what I believed. An hour later, I set the helicopter down on the helipad and unbuckled us both. *Time for the marking and claiming. Then she can never leave me.* No wolf to my knowledge had survived long away from their mate after being marked. Moon sickness soon followed, no different from that of a wolf who had never found their mate.

I helped Everly out of the helicopter and we ducked out of the way of the spinning blades. I picked her up and rushed to the lodge, taking the steps in a single bound. She lay against my chest and it filled me with pride. Now was our time.

"It's perfect," she said, taking in the living room with the huge stone fireplace, the overhead exposed beams of giant redwood and the spectacular picture window framing the valley below.

"Would you like anything? Are you hungry? Thirsty?"

"I'm everything, and I need a shower in the worst way."

"Go. Each bedroom has a bathroom, so take your pick. I'll shower and make us some food." Now that she was with me forever, I could take time to romance her, to let her know how very special she was to me, that she was my one.

"You cook? With all that staff at your command?"

"One specialty is all I can claim—a mean omelet."

Thirty minutes later, I had showered and had said omelet prepared and plated when she rejoined me.

She looked so beautifully clean and shiny, bundled up in a thick white robe, that it was all I could do not to fall on her and ravish every last thought right out of her sweet, curvy little body.

"Come. Eat."

"It smells so good." She dived in, downing a glass of orange juice between mouthfuls. I opened a bottle of champagne to celebrate, turning her drink into a mimosa.

"Nice. What shall we toast to?" she asked, picking up her champagne flute.

"To a wonderful night spent enjoying each other's company."

January Bain

"To tonight." We clinked glasses and locked eyes for a moment. She was in a good place now. Her eyes were clearer, stronger from the nourishment, and as wide and green as emerald pools. "Now what, Wolfie?" she taunted.

I was even starting to enjoy her use of the nickname. "Now we enjoy what nature intended."

"So romantic," she murmured with a shy grin.

I make a quick lunge for her.

The world blurred around me as Everly filled my senses. Her lips parted for me and I captured her mouth, my tongue twining with hers and making my cock pulse with the need to have those sweet lips wrapped around it.

"I love everything about you," I said. I pulled the tie on the robe, exposing her bare breasts, and kissed my way down her warm body. "I love this nipple, and this nipple, this belly button, these pussy lips, this clit, this highway to heaven."

She moaned as I slipped two fingers inside her and stroked her. "Mine," I said.

"Yours for tonight."

"And every night."

I picked her up and bore her to the master suite. I wanted her spread in front of me, pink and wet, and I wanted it now.

Chapter Twenty-Four

Everly

I ached for him, needing his touch as I'd never needed anything before him. When he laid me down before him on the bed as though I were a feast he had to consume, I found myself falling into him. So much power filled his hard body. I licked my lips at the remembered taste of him, at the feel of him taking me, of his hard body invading mine.

He pulled my legs wide apart and lowered himself between them. When he applied his mouth to my core, I bucked with the sensation. I fought to breathe, the hunger beating at me. My head thrashed back and forth as he sucked on my clit, then ran his gloriously thick and talented tongue up my channel, sweeping it back and forth, licking up all the wetness I spilled.

"So good. Don't stop," I moaned. I was dying. His tongue became raspier, setting my sensitive nerve endings ablaze. He reached up and pinched both my nipples. When he clamped down on my clit, I fell over

January Bain

into the abyss, spasms of deep pleasure radiating outward from my pussy. I shuddered for long moments, unable to think or reason.

When I opened my eyes, he was leaning over me, observing me intently.

"I love to watch you come," he murmured, his eyes alight with emotion.

"My turn," I commanded. "Lie down, Wolfie."

He smiled, then did as I asked, laying that beautiful body down beside me. Broad shoulders, hard biceps and golden flesh stretched across his chest and down his lean, muscular abs, filling my vision. Between his thighs, his engorged cock stood out from his body. He was exceptionally well endowed, heavily veined with length and girth to spare. And the best part was that no visible wounds remained from earlier. Just thinking of what could have happened fired my soul.

I leaned over him and took that magnificent cock between my far smaller hands. My lips parted when he pressed the wide head against them, my tongue catching the first drops of his peppery essence.

"That's it, *bella*, suck me." I looked up to see him staring at me, his expression savage with lust. I worked the mushroom-shaped tip, then in one swoop, captured all of him that I could, sucking harder. I pressed against the sensitive area under his cockhead and he bucked against my mouth.

I couldn't hold back my moans. When he tightened his fingers in my hair, pulling me away from what I desired, I mewled in protest.

"No, I want to come inside you. I can't wait any longer. I need to do this now."

He lifted me up and threw me down alongside him. He entered me without preamble, pushed himself deep inside me, part pleasure, part pain. He was thick, stretching me, working inside my snug entrance with firm, determined thrusts.

"Sweet, tight pussy," he crooned. "So hot... Take me, baby. Take all of me."

Panting cries fell from my lips and I arched my back to take him deeper, needing more, needing all of him. I was desperate for him, for this final time, to remember how amazing it was between us, like two stars that would collide and burn in an explosion of lust. Each lance of agonizing pleasure brought me spiraling closer and closer to that oblivion.

He pulsed larger still, making my channel ever more sensitive, using his hands to pull my ass to bring me in tighter. The connection between us — it was everything. When he buried himself to the hilt, I screamed, grinding into him. I felt every inch of his cock as it stretched me, throbbed inside me, pulled me wide open, pushing me nearly beyond endurance. My pussy rippled around him, each nerve ending blazing into brilliant life.

"Please...please..." I had no idea what I was begging for. All I could process was this exquisite excess of pleasure and pain and hunger.

His hips flexed, pressing his thick length inside me. Without warning, waves and waves of deeper pleasure sluiced through me with devasting results. The world vanished with the peaking of my extended orgasm. *Cataclysmic.* His release pulsed hotter than seemed possible...then something huge swelled inside me. Something I didn't understand, a hot flick of lightning-sharp sensations that went far beyond mere pleasure. He locked himself inside me, holding me tight against his hard chest and, almost unable to breathe, I sobbed out my ecstasy.

He used his teeth to graze my shoulder for a split second before he growled with what sounded like displeasure. *Or discomfort.*

I slowly became aware of my surroundings. He was inside me still, huge and hard, and I didn't understand how that could be.

"What's wrong, Cristaldo?" I whispered. I was satiated beyond belief, but uncertain of why I couldn't move. We seemed to be stuck together, his cock spasming inside my pussy. "What's going on?"

"It's called knotting. That always happens between mated pairs. My wolf wanted me to mark and claim you and now he won't let you go. I'm sorry. I couldn't do it. I couldn't lie to you again."

"You lied to me? After what I told you!" My anger burst to the surface. "How could you do that?" I tried to break away from him, but we were somehow still joined together. My pussy clenched with this exquisite suffering. Trapped, I glared up at him.

He had the grace to look chastised. "But I couldn't do it. That's the important thing. I stopped myself from marking you. Don't you see? I stopped. In time."

"What the hell is this marking thing?"

"I bite you, then forever after you hold my personal scent. All other wolves are warned off. It's how we claim our mates."

"And you couldn't do it. Why?" It was hard to make sense of this when my body was still orgasming, unable to stop. *Can one die from too many orgasms? Will people find us one day, still clutched in each other's arms?* I shook my head, trying to dispel the strange visual.

"I was going to. Had planned to. Then something you said stopped me, that if I lied to you again you would *never* give all of yourself to me. I want that—I don't want anything to stand between us." His tone was raw with emotion, begging me for understanding. He appeared almost broken, as though he were standing at the edge of a cliff, uncertain if the fall into me would end him. I had never felt more powerful...or more called upon to do the right thing.

I stared into those creamy brown eyes for a long time. My anger drained completely away and I saw the real Cristaldo, the timeless soul within the proud alpha. A man who had everything and commanded his world, and yet who had taken such an incredible chance. It left me vulnerable in return. My heart burst open, too full to contain such a thing. To think he wanted nothing to stand between us. That had always been my treasured wish to find in another, but was something I wasn't certain would ever happen for me, or even if it really happened for anyone.

"That is the most romantic and real thing I've ever heard anyone say. Thank you." I shifted a bit, the lock between us becoming too tight now, my flesh overstretched.

"Ah, but I'm not certain what to do now," he confessed.

"You mean we could be stuck like this? Forever?"

"Apparently so." His look said he was contrite, but his voice didn't agree. He sounded proud and free and very, very alpha.

I arched my eyebrows at him. "So, now that I have you in my clutches, so to speak, do you promise never to lie to me again, so help you God?"

He looked at me again, locking eyes with me. "I do. I promise never to lie to you again. No matter if I think it justified, I won't. But you must promise to keep my secrets, not to share them with your human family, or your new wolf family. No one." The final words held much significance for him. They rang with the importance of a distant bell tolling.

I made the biggest leap of faith in my life then. But all I had seen, what Cristaldo had let me see, had shared with me—it all gave me the strength to say what I said next. *Life-changing words.*

"Then bite me, Wolfie, so your wolf will be happy and let us go. Not that it doesn't feel divine to be so close, but I would like to be free to do other things with you sometime in this lifetime."

"Are you sure? Because once it's done, it can't be undone."

The air crackled between us.

It was hard to think, with us pressed together as one, but something told me that it would be okay. That this was the man for me. He'd changed for me, given up total control and let me inside his personal space. Given me all that I had asked for. I couldn't imagine what it had cost him. *An alpha.* How could I not do my part? Yes, it was fast, but it felt right. From the moment I'd met him, I'd sensed that he would change my life, but never had I thought it would be quite like this, this wide crack in my very existence that would change me forever. But I was already looking back at my former life. Scared? *Damn right.* But I was also electrified at all that was to come. Being with this exciting man, learning my heritage—it all loomed just in front of me, and it was time to grab it with both hands.

"Yes, I'm sure."

My breath stilled, knowing what that meant. It was a forever thing. Was I ready for this?

Before I could give it a second thought, he grasped me by the hips and bucked himself up from the bed, driving himself in and out of me in long and oh-so-satisfying strokes. His cock rubbed hard against my clit and I gushed with wetness, easing the way. He sucked one breast while teasing the other with his fingers. He drew tightly on a nipple and my pussy clenched him harder, desperate for release from this exquisite agony.

"Your cock was made for my loving," I said, breathless from bouncing up and down on my new favorite toy. I was so swollen that I had to come, to ease the throb. It was all I knew. All I could feel. I was out of control and sobbing my need aloud, gripping him harder to push him over the edge with me.

"This pussy is *mine*."

I struggled against him, grinding into him.

"Make it all yours," I said, my need for release taking over. The connection was too raw, too overwhelming.

"Say you want it. Surrender to me," he growled, pulling back, his hot breath teasing me.

"I want you. Mark me. Claim me." I knew the power as I said the words, because his expression turned to one of rapture and his dark eyes smoldered.

"I should make you wait as punishment for jumping into the pit with me tonight."

"Wouldn't you be punishing yourself as well?" I wiggled under him, trying to make him break his concentration and lose control.

It worked.

With a hard thrust, he pushed into me, seating himself fully, each inch filling me completely. My breath seized. He rocked into me in a frenzy, grabbing at my hips and pulling me closer.

I moaned, his wide girth sliding in and out in increasingly rapid strokes, our bodies making slick sounds as we came together. His shaft thickened and lengthened beyond belief, pushing me to the limits. I began to ripple with involuntary spasms, my muscles clenching around the invasion. A climax shot through my system. But it wasn't enough. Not nearly enough. My body became hotter, my senses maddened.

He destroyed me. Powerful, deep thrusts filled me, such exquisite pleasure that I could scarcely hold on. Stars exploded behind my tightly closed eyes and I dimly heard myself sobbing with ecstasy.

The sense of being stretched grew stronger, wilder, and an urge to be filled beyond my limit allowed it to happen. *The knotting.* I knew when we locked together, our bodies becoming one, that it was forever. There could be no holding back.

The air glimmered around us, sparkling with points of light.

He bit me then, on the shoulder. I jumped with the pain but eased when he licked lovingly over the spot. I opened my eyes to stare into his and I swore I could see eternity in their swimming depths.

"It is done. My beautiful love. We are Forever Mates. I love you more than I could ever have imagined possible."

"I've fallen in love with you, Cristaldo. So soon, I know, but I feel it. A commitment to be by your side for all the days of my life."

"And I promise to be true to you for all my time on this earth. To keep you safe and protected. To be only with you." His raw honesty and courage were on full display.

I brushed the tears from my eyes. His words had filled me with such emotion.

"I promise to be true to only you. To be your lover, your friend and your mate," I vowed.

"Thank you."

"For what?' I asked as he took up my hand and kissed each finger tenderly.

"For being you. You make me so proud to be with you."

And those darn waterworks started all over again. I dried my tears and found him looking at me with mischief riding high in those dreamy eyes of his.

"Now, let's go home and introduce you to everyone and have some fun," he said.

Yes, a new expanded family and community. I howled then, my very first howl, and the sound filled the desert and lifted up to kiss the sky. He joined me and we filled the night with our music and love and pledge to the future.

Want to see more from this author?
Here's a taster for you to enjoy!

Sin City Wolf: Howl
January Bain

Excerpt

Maximus

"Dearly beloved, we are gathered here today —"

Maximus vibrated with excessive energy, droning out the minister. Standing there like a stuffed turkey in his dove gray morning coat and tails waiting for his brother and mate to conclude the official ceremony, all he could think about was *sign the damn contract already*. The sooner he got out of this godawful monkey suit and had an extended run in the clear, crisp desert air, the better.

He stretched his neck under the stiff white collar. There wasn't much call for such attire in the sacred halls of a dusty library researching ancient writings, seeking clues to the whereabouts of sacred objects, in particular the House of Luceres' holiest of grails, the Lupus Sanguis Chalice. Just thinking of laying his hands on the priceless item made his heartbeat quicken.

Lives spent in the higher halls of learning was a calling he and his twin Alessandro were well suited to. He didn't want the unenviable job of being CEO of a string of worldwide casinos, like his soon-to-be married brother controlled, though he admired how his sibling managed the position with such style and grace.

But even Cristaldo had to release his wolf on occasion, to manage his beast effectively. Maximus hid a grin at the reminder of how off the rails his alpha sibling had become when he first met up with the lovely, all-too-human Everly. He'd nearly lost it, according to their brother Lucius — Cristaldo's twin — who took great glee in reminding everyone of the fact.

"And do you, Everly Joy Affini, take this man, Cristaldo Maximus Luceres, to be your lawfully wedded husband, until you are reborn?"

"I do."

The words sounded so final, albeit quite accurate, and were accompanied by a few notes of surprise from amongst the human wedding guests. They'd be even more shocked if they understood what it *truly* meant. That once a mated werewolf died after finding their Forever Mate, they reincarnated and came back and searched until they found each other. All they needed was a plan to meet up again, though the fragrance of their mate and the call of lust it created seemed to be sufficient in most cases. A fascinating world to be part of, one that would shock human sensibilities to their foundations. *Reason why we have to live in secret among them. Pack rule number one.*

"And do you, Cristaldo Maximus Luceres, take this woman, Everly Joy Affini, to be your lawfully wedded wife, until you are both reborn?"

"I do."

My brother raised his mate's veil and the look of adoration and love so clear in his eyes made Maximus glance away.

A sense of need and envy stirred deep inside him, its rawness taking him by surprise. *What is this?* He ran a finger between his shirt collar and his neck in an effort to loosen it. Taking a deep breath, he forced himself to remain still and see the final part of the ceremony to its expected conclusion. His twin Alessandro stirred at his side, apparently needing a deep breath of his own. The church was too hot and too stifling by half.

He held on, encouraged by a vision in his mind's eye of the pair of them racing across the desert floor, the crescent moon overhead lighting the way. He couldn't even begin to think of him and Alessandro finding their Forever Mate, though she haunted their dreams on occasion. The one who would love them both. Did she even exist?

His mind revisited an intoxicating scent he'd experienced for a couple of brief seconds a few months back while visiting their holdings in Milan. *Who was that female?* The fragrance had vanished before he could track her, an annoyance that still plagued him.

"You may now kiss your bride." The gleam in the minister's eyes expressed his understanding of who they were and the importance of the pair he was joining together for all eternity. Of course — he was their father, Cesare, home with their mother, Sophia, from traveling abroad. Their entire extended community was in attendance as well, from all corners of the globe. More than two hundred in total from their side of the family alone sat patiently, and some — mostly the male attendees — impatiently in the pews.

I have to get out of here.

Soon, bro. There's time between the ceremony and the reception for a good run.

The clock began to tick ever louder in his head. If it were just supernatural beings present, he could get away with leaving before the bride and groom made their way down the aisle to be greeted by well wishers and rice. But humans, they were a different matter.

By the time his father had finished his blessing of the newly married pair and the documents were signed, his entire body felt about to vanish into one of the multiverses where they became wolves…and this time not come back. *Run forever free on the other side.*

Not that he had caught more than a glimpse of that special dimension in his decades plus of shifting. He'd studied the phenomenon of course, understanding that in physics energy was never lost and that werewolves became altered at the quantum level due to their special DNA.

He imagined explaining *that* to a physics professor at the Sapienza in Rome where he and his twin were currently scholars in residence. But understanding it and preventing it were two different things. He had no more control at times than a chameleon that changed color in a new environment, especially when the full moon called.

A new energy in the air woke him from his musings. The agony was over and everyone were moving, following the newly married pair down the red carpet to the open doorway. He took a big breath of fresh air into his starved lungs outside the church doors, watching the crowd mill about, vying for their chance to speak to the happy couple.

"Let's nab the copter before anyone else gets the same idea," Maximus said, jerking off his black tie and thrusting it into his jacket pocket. Undoing a few buttons on his white shirt front, his muscles tight with the urgent need to release the pent-up strain of the past few days, he thumped his twin on the back. Alessandro stood beside him on the church steps, his expression calm. He'd always been the more patient one, from the moment of birth when he let his twin go first. "Let's go."

Less than ten minutes later, they buckled themselves into the seats of the helicopter. It was gassed and ready, perched like a sleek beast on the roof of the Glitter Palace casino.

Maximus took over the controls, setting course for the vast desert property the pack also owned near Sin City. Not that his twin was any less proficient, but Alessandro tended to let him lead, a situation that alleviated brotherly rivalries...most of the time.

"Perhaps we'll be next," Alessandro mused, his expression distant when Maximus glanced over at him.

He snorted at the idea while keeping a close eye on the numerous gauges that lined the cockpit. "Not bloody likely, bro. Not many women want two men in their bed. At least, not many that will admit it. Besides, she'll like me best once I show her my considerable assets." He added a wolfish grin for good measure, wanting to ensure his twin didn't experience the slump that the festivities tended to bring to unmated pack members.

"It's not what you have bro, it's knowing *how* to use it. And it's not all about the cock. Your tongue can be mightier. And my talent in that direction is legendary."

The reply surprised him. This mate they spoke of was a fantasy, and yet here was his brother testing him.

"When she takes *my knot*, it'll be all over but the fat lady singing."

Alessandro remained quiet while he set down the whirlybird on the pad and killed the motor. Unbuckling his harness, Maximus reminded them why they were there. "Mate or no mate, time to hunt."

"Oh yeah, you're on."

They both jumped to the ground and began shedding their clothing as if they were on fire. When Alessandro was naked, his warrior body revealed in all its glory in the moonlight, from his wide chest to his muscled abs to his strong thighs, Maximus knew he was seeing a mirror image of himself. A very satisfying image. They also had in common thick dark hair that refused to be tamed and cocks that wouldn't quit.

But now was the time to be free. Anticipation took over and he embraced the change. In seconds, he was through the portal that glinted with sparks of light when he entered it, every energetic cell of his body shifting to a new form, before he was thrown back through again.

Changed. To a wolf.

He stretched and blinked, his keen senses honed to a deadly sharpness. He lifted his muzzle to catch the faint breeze, testing, hungry for distraction. The forest floor was enhanced with his new vision, mutated to an array of shades unknown to the human eye. Subtle hues of blacks, browns and grays. Movements of tiny creatures caught his attention before he caught the scent of a deer.

This way.

He led the chase, his big paws closing the distance in leaps and bounds. It was good to be wolf. So good that he allowed himself the luxury of a resounding howl of wolf song, meant to tighten the senses of all creatures of the desert.

You'll frighten our prey away.

He didn't like the reminder. Sure, he was spontaneous at times, but it beat taking too long to make a decision—one of Alessandro's characteristics that could bite them in the ass one day if he hesitated at the wrong moment.

There will be lots of others, bro, stand down.

He used his powerful body to give his sibling a solid nudge on the upper shoulder. Alessandro hit back, harder than he had.

Bring it on. Sibling rivalry helped keep them in top physical form and he was more than ready for the challenge.

Their hard bodies twisted and slammed together with a loud resounding thud, both of them hitting the hard-packed sand as one snarling, swirling mass of limbs and fur. He fought hard, looking for an opening. All he needed was a slight pause in action where he could take his brother down. *Make him submit.* Seconds ticked by as each sought the advantage, strutting and sending out telepathic taunts.

I have the bigger knot.

I have the most talented tongue.

The wrestling match, fueled by the week's limiting formal events, continued unabated for far longer than usual. Maximus began to realize neither of them could win without doing the other harm. And that was not the point. But still they fought, past the time they should have stopped. *The lust for a mate.* That was the culprit at the base of this primal drive. Maximus sensed this even as he couldn't stop himself from trying to assert his alpha pride over his brother's.

His flanks shuddering with exhaustion, he locked his jaws onto the back of Alessandro's neck to get him under control.

A loud, long growl of warning caused him to break his hold in an instant. He tensed and peered into the darkness, legs bracing for combat with the intruder. Alessandro stood at his side, prepared as well to rise to the challenge. Over there, near a Joshua tree, a gleam of bright blue eyes— *A third wolf.* And behind him other dark shadows appeared, eyes gleaming in the darkness, a solid line of danger.

Home of Erotic Romance

Sign up for our newsletter and find out about all our romance book releases, eBook sales and promotions, sneak peeks and FREE romance books!

About the Author

January Bain has wished on every falling star, every blown-out birthday candle and every coin thrown in a fountain to be a storyteller. To share the tales of high adventure, mysteries, and full-blown thrillers she has dreamed of all her life. The story you now have in your hands is the compilation of a lot of things manifesting itself for this special series. Hundreds of hours spent researching the unusual and the mundane have come together to create a series that features strong women who don't take life too seriously, wild adventures full of twists and unforeseen turns, and hot complicated men who aren't afraid to take risks. She can only hope the stories of her beloved Brass Ringers will capture your imagination as much as they did hers when she wrote them.

If you are looking for January Bain, you can find her hard at work every morning without fail in her office with two furry babies trying to prove who does a better job of guarding the doorway. And, of course, she's married to the most romantic man! Who once famously replied to her inquiry about buying fresh flowers for their home every week, "Give me one good reason why not?" Leaving her speechless and knocking her head against the proverbial wall for being so darn foolish. She loves flowers.

January loves to hear from readers. You can find her contact information, website details and author profile page at https://www.totallybound.com

www.ingramcontent.com/pod-product-compliance
Lightning Source LLC
Chambersburg PA
CBHW020419180626
46812CB00003B/1054